Duffy
The Tale
of a Terrier

Happy Tails!

Gary Porter

Duffy

The Tale of a Terrier

GARY PORTER

BEAVER'S
POND
PRESS

Illustrations by Greg Holcomb

ISBN 10: 1-59298-369-3
ISBN 13: 978-1-59298-369-8

Library of Congress Catalog Number: 2011923176

Printed in the United States of America

First Printing: 2011

15   14   13   12   11   5   4   3   2   1

Graphic design by James Monroe Design, LLC.

Beaver's Pond Press, Inc.
7104 Ohms Lane, Suite 101
Edina, MN 55439—2129
(952) 829-8818
www.BeaversPondPress.com

To order, visit www.BeaversPondBooks.com
or call (800) 901-3480. Reseller discounts available.

With love to Melissa
In honor of Polly
and
In memory of Duffy and Daisy

"The dog is a gentleman;
I hope to go to his heaven, not man's."

—Mark Twain

Letter to W.D. Howells, April 2, 1899

CONTENTS

DUFFY

PRO-DOGUE

Humans don't have tails. We dogs do. Of course, there are plenty of other differences between us. People walk around on two legs, a vertical approach to life. Ours is a more horizontal take, trotting around on all fours as we do. What I found during my life was there is much we have in common, and nothing about all we share is more important than the love we have for each other. This tale is the story of all that I shared with the two most important humans in my life. You might say that it is the tale of one pooch's life with dog's best friend.

"Nice to meet you, Rex. This may seem like a silly question, but where in h-e-double-hockey sticks am I?"

"You're not. In fact, it's just the opposite. Welcome to paradise."

One

HEAVEN

The last mental picture I have from down "there" was of me marching around the vet's office with this tube sticking out of my leg, all the while dragging around some contraption with a bottle on it. The only way I could have looked sillier was if they had adorned me in one of those hospital gowns, the type open in the back for practical purposes. Though my accompaniments seemed a bit odd, I wasn't the type to get too lathered up. The worried looks on the faces of my folks told me they felt otherwise.

I should probably say a word or two about my use of the somewhat folksy expression "my folks." Humans who choose to live with dogs go by many different names. I always cringed at the term "owner" as if we dogs were mere possessions, sort of like an accessory; although of course we have all seen those toy dogs who are reduced to a life inside some movie star's handbag. Equally objectionable to me was the term "master" as if we were in servitude to humans. To me, the two people who put a roof over my head were my adoptive parents, affectionately known from here on out in the plural as "my folks" and in the singular as "Mom" and "Dad."

Back to the matter at hand: My only concern was what in the heck had happened to my morning meal. I always took my breakfast bright and early and here it was in the middle of the day and no chow yet. Come to find out, I was being readied for some surgery. I won't burden you with all of the gory details, but some tests showed that I had a nasty lump on my liver that needed to come out.

When I woke up during the night after surgery my surroundings didn't look much like a vet's office. Instead, as far as the eye could see was row after row of bowls filled with every kind of food known to dogkind. Small bits, big bits, bacon bits—you name it—all you had to do was walk down the rows and pick out whatever tickled your fancy. And the biggest barrel of rawhides you could imagine.

Where could this be?

Where were my folks?

Well, it didn't take me long to figure out that I

was somewhere quite different than that vet's office.

In the end, I didn't survive the "post-op." All went well during the surgery to remove the lump but, sometime during the night in the recovery room, my heart just gave out. I suppose that meeting my maker in this fashion was a bit ironic since I had been giving out my heart to my folks my whole life.

Never mind where I was. I was famished. I dug into the biggest helping of chow I had ever seen, only coming up for air once I licked the bowl clean. Having satisfied my most basic of needs, I turned back to consider my current surroundings. I began to realize where I wasn't. This wasn't the kind of place where I had spent my first fourteen years. I know humans are fond of naming everything. And whatever name you might give to this place, I was definitely somewhere quite different now.

As part of my daily ritual I gave myself a good licking, a dog's version of a morning shower. With that bit of personal hygiene out of the way, I trotted over to find a comfortable spot in the shade of a big oak tree. Normally I would have been out like a light within minutes. Instead I was wide awake. Let's face it. Already I missed these two humans with whom I had spent nearly my entire life.

The idea kept coming back to me. I needed to put

my thoughts about my life down on paper. Certainly that would have been something I wasn't capable of down there, but up here there seemed to be no boundaries. And the more I considered it, the more I realized that I needed to tell my life's story and get it in the hands of my folks. After all our years together I knew that my leaving must have been one of the toughest things they ever faced.

About this time, up trots a very handsome member of my own species.

"Well, hello there, old chap! Welcome to paradise!"

"Thank you. The name is Duffy, but friends call me Duff."

"Pleased to meet you, Duff. I'm Rex."

"Nice to meet you, Rex. I know this may seem like a silly question, and pardon the vernacular, but where in the h-e-double-hockey sticks *am* I?"

"You're not," Rex replied.

"I'm sorry, but what did you say?" I asked, puzzled.

"You are nowhere in hell. In fact, just the opposite and, as I said, welcome to paradise. You obviously led a good life. And by that I do mean *a* good life, not *the* good life. Too often, it is leading *the* good life that lands so many poor souls down below rather than up here," he explained, nodding his head slightly down and then up.

Catching my breath, I gave some thought to what Rex said and then I realized my suspicions were correct. I was no longer on Earth and had entered somewhere quite different. Quite different indeed.

Rex said he would be glad to show me around later and even help me find my birth mother, someone I hadn't seen since a few weeks after I came into the world. As daunting a task as that seemed to me at the time, he explained how easy it would be, and that this was only one of the many amazing things about this place.

Turns out Rex and I were related. He a Boston Terrier, me a Terrier mix. The years in the afterlife had been good to Rex. He had the shiniest coat I had ever seen on a dog. Rex attributed this to the top-of-the-line dog food he ate from the first day he arrived up here. Combine the shiny coat with the distinctive black-and-white coloring of his breed, and he looked like he was dressed for his own wedding. He even had a tail to go with his tuxedo, though it was a curly little appendage. Rex had an air of confidence and nobility about him.

"So, Rex, I want to write my life's story and send it in a letter to my folks back on Earth. I know that may seem a bit far-fetched, but do you know of any way to make that happen?"

"Well, to be honest, old chap, there are few constraints on anything one wants to do up here. But wouldn't your folks already know your life story? I assume you lived with them for most of your life, did you not?"

"We had thirteen years together, the three of us. But you have to understand, I was adopted and there were parts of my life, leading up to my rescue, that they had no way of knowing about. Let's just say I had a *ruff* start in life and I would like to let my folks know just how appreciative I was that they rescued me and loved me unconditionally for the rest of my life. If only I could reassure them that I have landed in a safe place up here."

"So you spent some time in a shelter, did you, Duff? I've heard some horror stories about those places."

The way Rex emphasized *those places* made me wonder exactly what it was he knew about shelters.

"Yeah, I sure did. But this shelter wasn't so bad. The people there treated me well and did everything they could to find me a permanent home. Still, I can't tell you what a relief it was the day I left for my new home. I just know the folks must be grieving something awful after all our time together. I was thinking my letter might help them with the healing process."

"Catharsis," Rex responded.

"Ca...what?" I turned to him in complete bewilderment.

"Catharsis. That's what humans call it when they find ways to cope with the grieving process. You think your letter to your folks would be cathartic to them."

I was beginning to understand that my new friend was no ordinary dog. Here was a learned canine, one with a vocabulary to match his formal black-and-white attire.

"Yes, yes. I want to help them with their catharsis," I replied, trying my best to keep pace with Rex.

"I can understand your motivation, Duff. But why not take it a step further and put this story of yours down in a book, one that could be shared with everyone down there, not just your folks?"

"Gosh, Rex, I never thought of that. Why would I want to share my life's story with the entire human race?"

"Duff, take a long look around you. See those rows and rows of chow, the kind that I assume you gorged yourself on, the same thing all the dogs do on their arrival. You need to understand that we operate up here on a communal system, everyone pitching in to do their parts."

"So what does any of this have to do with me writing a book, Rex?" So far I wasn't sure how to connect the dots on what the old boy was trying to tell me.

"Royalties. You sell your book and you get a percentage of the take. Royalties. They could be your meal ticket. Literally."

I knew little about royalties but with the mere mention of the word *meal* I reacted in a way you might expect from Pavlov's dog. Now, Rex had my undivided attention. But still I had doubts about my literary leanings.

"Rex, to be perfectly honest, I know nothing about writing a book. I am confident I could tell my story, but who in their right mind would publish a book written by a dog? And, even if I was a human, and it is pretty obvious I am not, don't most of the two-leggeds who write books eventually have to hook up with an agent? Where in the world—sorry, I mean *Heaven*—would I find an agent?"

Rex just stared at me with those bug-like eyes that make his breed so distinctive. Then he gave me a look that I will never forget. I was going to say one I will never forget even if I live to be a hundred, but then

I caught myself. All the while he just kept staring at me until I finally asked him somewhat indignantly what was so peculiar about my question regarding an agent. His answer made perfectly good sense.

"Think about it, Duff. Haven't you ever heard that all of the good agents are from out East? And though New York might beg to differ, don't you suppose some of the very best are from Boston?"

I had found my perfect partner in the form of Rex the Boston Terrier in the dapper black-and-white tuxedo. Or so I thought. Before very long, it became evident that Rex wanted to be more than just my agent.

Later that same day I had just started to make some headway on my story when he came sauntering up behind me. "What are you writing there, old chap?"

Annoyed the first couple of times at his way of greeting me, I eventually learned not to take Rex's moniker for me personally. It had nothing to do with my advanced age and was just a reflection of his East Coast roots. In fact, Rex referred to all of his acquaintances up here as "old chaps."

"Just getting going on my story," I told him.

"So, did you decide yet on a genre?"

"Come again?" I asked, puzzled yet again.

"You know, a genre. What *kind* of story is this

going to be?"

"Well, I mean it to be my life's story," I quickly retorted.

"So, I take it that this will be nonfiction, rather than fiction, is that right?"

I hesitated briefly, not wanting to admit to Rex that I always mixed up the two. *Let me think.* Now nonfiction, does that mean it is true or does it mean that it is not true? Darn. I never could keep these straight and here I am talking to the canine equivalent of the editor-in-chief of *The New Yorker*.

Taking his bait, I went out on a limb and replied, "Yeah, that's right, nonfiction."

"Okay. Fine. But you have to understand, old chap, there are many variations on nonfiction. For instance, there are autobiographies; there are memoirs; there are personal essays. So which kind of nonfiction is this meant to be?"

"Well, I always thought when people told the story of their life, that those were called autobiographies. So that must be it. I am writing my autobiography!"

Pleased with my definitive response, I listened intently for Rex's reply.

"Okay, we could consider an autobiography. You know, many years ago there was this horse who wrote his life story. He called it *Black Beauty, The Autobiography of a Horse*. But these days it seems that autobiographies are only written by famous people, politicians, celebrities, the jet-setters of the world. You weren't a jet-setter down there, were you, Duff?"

"Never stepped paw on a plane in my life. No way this 'earth' dog was going to get that far off the ground," I replied. "So, how about calling it a memoir? I assume one of those has to do with memories, what someone remembers about his life experiences."

"Better be careful with a memoir, old chap."

"What's to be careful with?" I snapped back, starting to show just the slightest bit of irritation with my Terrier friend's third-degree interrogation.

"It's just that lately I have been hearing some disturbing things about these so-called memoirs. Writers claiming that certain things happened to them when most of them led pretty ordinary lives. The pressure comes from publishers who think you need to have some juice if you are going to sell a memoir. So some guy claims he led a life of ruin, depravity, decadence, and debauchery, and puts it all in a memoir. Next thing he is on the talk show circuit, telling the whole world about it. Well, on closer scrutiny, it turns out most of his claims just weren't true, and all hell breaks loose. Why? Fabrications."

"Why would a writer fabricate...make things up?" I asked, now that Rex had my undivided attention.

"Oh, I suppose to help sell books. To satisfy the public's insatiable desire for dirt."

"Well, being a Terrier, I do know a thing or two about digging up dirt, but I sure don't intend to do any fabricating," I snapped back, a bit offended that Rex would lump me in with those characters.

It was becoming more and more clear to me that my new agent was the meddling kind. I thought I had signed on with an *agent* but now I had an *editor* thrown in to boot. I guess you could call my new relationship with Rex a package deal.

Knowing that most of us Terriers have some bulldog bred into us, I shouldn't have been surprised when Rex plowed onward without even taking a breath. "You have to understand, Duff, it's just that when I take your book to one of the big publishing houses out East, the first question they will ask me is about the genre. I know you could care less, but they have to know where it fits. Publishers like to pigeon-hole everything. When it comes down to it, they want to know what shelf it will go on at Barnes and Noble."

By now it was obvious that Rex took this whole genre business pretty seriously. I decided I better play along. "Well, if this is nonfiction and you don't want to call it my autobiography and you think we should steer clear of a memoir, then what are the other choices?"

For the longest time Rex said nothing. He walked around with that bullet head of his down, obviously deep in thought. When he finally looked up, those beady eyes fixed on me and out it came.

"I've got it! We will call it a tale. A tale is a story, an account, a yarn. This way we don't have to get all hung up on how much is true and how much is bogus. This will simply be one dog laying out a good story about something. You know, the way Mark Twain told his tales of Tom Sawyer and Huck Finn. And how much better could it get? Here is a dog telling a tale, and what do all dogs have? We all have tails!"

Not wanting to burst his bubble, I hesitated before responding to what Rex obviously considered a brilliant idea. Hadn't he inspected me closely when we first met, the way dogs do? I had yet to meet another of my species who didn't pay particularly close attention to the back end of every dog they met, sniffing away until they were sure this one was to be trusted. Had he not observed that all I had was a stub, not a real tail?

"Uh, Rex, I don't know if you really noticed, but when it comes to the posterior, I got the proverbial short end of the stick, or shall we say short end of the tail."

Without even coming up for air, Rex blurted out, "Perfect! Don't you see the irony, old chap? A dog without much of the one thing we all have, a tail, and here he is telling his tale! Readers just love writers who can alliterate, so we will call your masterpiece very simply: *Duffy: The Tale of a Terrier*!"

"But how did you know my momma delivered eight of us little Terriers, Rex?"

"I had no clue of the number of offspring and I'm afraid you've lost me, old chap."

"A litter of eight. You said something about readers liking writers from a litter of eight and that was the exact number of us siblings, including Yours Truly!"

Rex gave me a look like I had just popped in from another planet, which was of course precisely what I just did. But ever the tactful one, he drew a long breath and tried to explain.

"Oh, now I see the source of confusion, Duff. I said readers like writers who *can* 'alliterate,' not those who *came* from 'a litter of eight'! You see, logical as it might seem, to alliterate has nothing to do with litters, or for that matter the numeral eight. It means using words in a sentence that have the same initial sound. *Tale of a Terrier* has just that sound, wouldn't you say?"

To illustrate for my tutor that I grasped this wonderful notion of alliteration, I felt like blurting out that I was an *em*barrassed *im*becile, but I decided not to belabor the point.

"Okay, Rex, *The Tale of a Terrier* suits me just fine," I responded, glad to have this whole nonsense about genre finally put to bed.

But Rex the wonder dog was on a roll and seemed happy to have me as his pupil in Creative Writing 101. "Now, Duff, one last point before you get down to business. You need to have a distinctive voice. Have you thought about the voice you intend to use?"

Once again, I was starting to wonder if I had bitten off more on the old rawhide than I could chew. "Sorry, Rex, but you're going to have to help me on this voice thing. Naturally, I never talked down there, and the closest I came to a voice was the bark I registered to alert the folks to any impending danger, you know, a delivery man approaching the house or a squirrel climbing up one of our trees. What do you mean, my 'voice'?"

Doing his best to hide his amusement at my apparent naïveté, Rex tried to lay it out for his independent study. "Okay, every writer telling his story must have a distinctive voice. Something that sets him apart from the pack. There are a couple of things that have a direct impact on whether one's voice is distinctive or not. First, you need to decide on the point of view of your story and, given the personal nature of what you intend to tell, I would recommend the story be told from your own point of view. But then you still have to decide whether your story will be told in first dog, second dog, or third dog."

Again, those beady eyes were fixed on me. I wouldn't have been surprised if Rex had a ruler waiting for a rap on the knuckles if I didn't give the right answer. But you can't fake complete and utter ignorance, so I answered in the only way I knew how: "Rex, I don't have a clue what you are talking about; could you please give me an example?"

"Sure, old chap. Say you and your people are out for a walk and the poodle of your dreams is approaching from the other direction. You could describe this in the first dog as 'I looked up just in time to see the poodle of my dreams trotting towards me.' Well, this same scene could be described in the third dog by simply saying, 'He looked up just in time to see the poodle of his dreams trotting towards him.' Or, finally, the less frequently used second-dog version would go something like, 'You look up just in time to see the poodle of your dreams trotting towards you.' Do you see the differences? Which do you think would work the best for your tale?"

"Yes, Rex, I see now what this whole fuss is all about and I would like to tell my story in the first dog. If I am going to describe the sensation of seeing the poodle of my dreams, I would rather be the one to do it and not leave the description of such a pleasurable experience to some second or third dog."

Whether or not this was the response he was looking for, I sensed that Rex figured it had already been a long day and that this would be a good time to end the tutorial. Maybe it was those beady eyes rolling around in his head like lottery balls in one of those cages that gave me that impression. At any rate, it *had* been a long day and at this point all I really wanted to do was find a place to bed down for the night. But I did have one last question for the little guy.

"Rex, I just have to ask you one other thing. How is it that you know so much about the publishing business?"

"Well, I have always been intrigued by the literary world and it certainly didn't hurt to be raised in the business. But that is for another day, old chap, so I bid you a good evening."

As Rex turned and trotted down the road, I

suddenly realized what a perfect pair we made. Here was this dog with the business acumen of a Wall Street banker and the literary leanings of a Hemingway, and here I was with a story to tell. So what follows is a tale, but not my tail. I am going to keep to myself the little bit of stub I do have left. My tale begins in the beginning and ends that fateful day in the vet's office.

Terriers dig. If we were meant to swim we
would have been born with fins.

Two
AND EARTH

The first and foremost thing to understand about me is that I was a Terrier. I tipped the scales at about forty pounds, placing me somewhere in size between one of those high-voltage Jack Russell Terriers and those muscle-bound Bull Terriers.

The word *terrier* comes from the Latin *terra*, which means "earth." So there you have it. I was an earth dog and this tells you nearly everything you need to know about me. I always had my nose to the ground, smelling and sniffing in hopes of flushing something out. No rabbit, squirrel, or any other four-legged critter out in the wild was ever safe when I was on its trail.

Terrier or earth dog also tells you what I *wasn't*. I never fancied myself as a water dog. Frankly, I got very jittery around lakes, rivers, or any other body of H_2O, and stayed clear of them. Put me on solid ground and give me a trail to follow, and I was as happy as a clam. Okay, wrong analogy, since they live in the sea and I just stated my feelings about water. Put me on solid ground and give me a trail to follow and I was happy as a pig in slop.

While I always considered myself a Terrier, a purebred I wasn't. Again, humans have names for everything. Call me a mutt, a mongrel, a cur, a Heinz 57, a mixed breed. None of these ever offended me, although my folks always preferred to put a positive spin on my pedigree, referring to me as a "mix."

As a mix I defied labels. I truly was one of a kind. All of the attention could be embarrassing at times. I couldn't go anywhere without someone calling out to my folks, "What *kind* of dog is he anyway?"

I suppose this question came up so frequently because of my unusual—I like to think of it as handsome—appearance.

Start with the ears. These were the first thing you would see looking at me head on. My ears always stood at perfect attention, as if I was a young cadet in my first day at West Point. And there wasn't much in the way of sound that those ears missed.

The ears and the rest of the head were a mix of black and tan, with the exception of a white stripe running down the center of my head and ending in a white nose. In contrast to the black and tan head, my nose looked like it had been stuck in the proverbial paint can. And the stitching on the nose. Just like what you see on a baseball. Three very nicely aligned rows of stitching ran on each side of the snout. I was never sure why I had the fancy sew job on the end of my nose, but it certainly added to my distinctive appearance.

Now we come to what *really* gave me a distinctive look. The easiest way to describe what came next is to recall the question my folks heard a thousand times over when showing off our family picture. And yes, we did have a family picture taken. Why, you might ask? Well, every year Mom raised money for the walkathon sponsored by the shelter where we first met (i.e., where I was biding my time until I found a proper home). The top fundraisers received a prize. And wouldn't you know, one year the prize Mom won was a sitting with a pet photographer.

What would prompt either Mom or Dad to whip out the family picture to show to a perfect stranger? It was usually in response to the standard question, "Do you have any children?"

Barely before the person finished asking the question, out came our family picture from either Mom's or Dad's wallet, with the qualifier, "Well...we have a four-legged son."

I always found that a sort of peculiar way to put it. Think of the last time someone asked you about your family. Did you respond, "Well, yes, we have a two-legged son who is a senior in high school and he is trying to decide between Yale and Harvard"? I think not.

Where was I? You will have to forgive me. I do tend to ramble and get off the point now and then, but it is usually because I find the ways of humans a bit odd at times. Oh yes, I was describing what it was that gave me such a distinctive look. My folks never tired of hearing the observation that so often followed when they showed off our family picture: "He looks like he is wearing a turtleneck!"

Now what an absurd idea—a dog wearing a turtle-neck sweater!

But time and again, that would be the first thing that came to someone's mind when they saw my mugshot. I suppose it was because as soon as your eyes scanned from that black and tan head, the next thing to come into view was a nearly pure white body, broken only by an occasional black spot. The spots were certainly not as prominent as on one of those firehouse dogs—I believe humans call them Dalmatians—but nonetheless they were there. People looking at that picture would swear that I was wearing a white turtleneck.

My belly was another attention grabber. Modesty aside, there is something divine about rolling on one's back on a freshly mowed lawn, which of course exposes that very revealing underside of one's anatomy. Although I never thought of it as much of a compliment, my folks always thought my belly was similar to that on a pig. You know, the tint of pink. In fact, one of their silly nicknames for me was Pink Belly.

Last, and in my case also least, was the aforementioned tail. As Rex would say, "Pure irony, old chap."

Some dog with a tail shorter than his snout telling his life story and he subtitles it *The Tale of a Terrier*. Oh, I have quite a tale to tell, you see, just not much of a tail. Nothing more than a stub. My tail had been docked.

According to Webster, a dock is the solid part of an animal's tail. Thus, a docked tail on a dog is that part remaining after the rest has been cut off. Like so many words in the English language, the word "dock" sometimes has an alternative meaning. Dock can be used to refer to the withholding of wages of an employee, e.g., "We had to dock Joe's wages because he is such a derelict and constantly shows up late for work." Well, I would like to dock the wages of whomever it was that had the bright idea to dock my tail.

On the other hand, what good is a tail? Humans seem to be no worse for the wear without them. No question they can get in the way. Assume for a minute that you are a dog at a party, one of those gatherings where everyone stands around and tries to act interested in what someone next to them is saying. A long-lost friend calls out your name from across the room. "Oh, Rusty, soooo maaaarvelous to see you."

You quickly turn to see who it is, and wham, through no fault of your own you knock off the shelf an expensive crystal vase with that dreadful tail of yours. No matter how gracious your hostess is, it is unlikely you will be invited back to one of her parties anytime in the near future. Assuming an active social life, this is the sort of thing that dogs sporting a tail have to worry about all the time. Not me. I never shattered a single piece of china or crystal in my fourteen years.

The little stub I did have, my docked tail, was actually more of a conversation piece than anything else. Come to think of it, a perfect ice breaker at one of those parties, especially if you are trying to grab the attention of someone of the opposite sex. Say, the cutest little spaniel—one of those with the adorable ears—walks up to you and exclaims, "What in the world happened to your tail anyway?"

Well, you have the ideal opening to wow her with your doghood: "Oh, many years ago I was chasing a fox and, as we Terriers will do, I had my head buried in a hole into which the coward had retreated. The next thing I know a fox-in-waiting clamps his razor-like incisors onto my beautiful foot-long tail and reduces it to nothing more than a stub with a single chomp." How adventurous this would sound to Spanky the Spaniel.

Enough about me. I need to move along with my story and not risk boring anyone to death with too much detail about my outwardly appearance. For the visual learner, I have included a snapshot on the flap of the book, just one of the couple thousand that Mom took of me over the years.

To sum it all up, without yapping my own horn too much, I guess you could say that I was an earth dog for all seasons: black on the head and ears, to match the rich soil of summertime; brown around the nose, the color of autumn leaves; white on the body, like a blanket of fresh snow on a bright winter's day; and, finally, pink on my belly, the color of blossoms in the spring.

**Just because you're born in a barn
doesn't mean you want to spend the
rest of your life in one.**

Three

RUFF START

Try to recall that first mental snapshot you have of your start in life. Now try to think how old you must have been at that time. Was it something from kindergarten that you can recollect? Maybe a faint image of that favorite blanket you dragged to school for nap time? As I look back now on my own life, it isn't something from kindergarten I remember, as I never bothered with such menial training. More on my formal education later.

My grand entrance into this life took place on a farm—to be specific, in a hayloft. There were eight of us in the litter. We were all cute as bugs, lying up in the mow, sucking our mother's milk, happy to play the parts of piglets and let our momma be the sow. Like so many of my species, I never knew my biological father. He was the classic rolling stone. In fact,

DUFFY

I couldn't even tell you what breed of dog my dad was. Mom herself was a mix and if I had to guess, my hunch is that my father probably was as well.

When you start mixing mixes with mixes, who knows what the result might be? I would like to think that all of that mixed blood had something to do with my handsome looks. At any rate, we were quite a sight: eight little squirts all huddled around our mom out there in the hayloft.

Aside from that mental image of all of us together as a family, the rest of what I remember from that farm isn't very pleasant. I am not sure how long it was after I was born, but looking back I imagine I was just a few weeks old. Early one morning the farmer came to the hayloft with his young son. My guess is that the young lad was about ten in human years. I could smell the fresh manure on their boots from the morning chores. It soon became obvious that the farmer wasn't in the best of moods.

"Gull dang, Jimmy. I knew we should have tied up that mongrel in the barn and not let her run wild. Now what are we going to do with eight more mouths to feed? We are trying to run a dairy farm here, not a halfway house for dogs. I told you when these pups were born that we would keep them as long as they could suck off their mom's teats and that would be it. Well, the day is fast approaching when her milk gives out and then what?" And with that soliloquy the farmer let loose a stream of tobacco juice that had been bubbling up in his mouth for who knows how long.

"I don't know," said young Jimmy as he held back tears, "but we have to do something. We need to find homes for them."

"Listen, we've had that sign in the front yard for six weeks now and not a single person has come by to even look at them. Now where are we going to find homes for these eight runts? No one is going to take any of these pups off our hands if they have to shell out money just to keep them fed."

To this day I can't tell you why I did what I did next. Let's just say I had a hunch—a gut feeling that what the farmer had in mind for me and my siblings wasn't going to be pleasant. Maybe it was the pitch-fork that he was leaning on that gave me a clue as to his intentions.

All of the other little guys seemed content to continue sucking Momma's milk. Not me. I gave my mother one last sorrowful glance and then made my run for daylight. The daylight came from a narrow opening in the big barn door in the hayloft. I leapt from the second floor, my ears flapping in the breeze on my descent.

For an instant I felt suspended in time and space. But just for an instant. I nearly had the wind knocked out of me when I landed one story down from the only home I had known to this point in my young life. Lucky for me the ground was covered in a fresh blanket of snow that helped to soften my free fall.

Once I had regained my senses I looked up to the door of the loft, hoping that my brothers and sisters would follow. But not a one of them did. The farmer glanced down at me with a disgusted look, tobacco juice still dribbling from the side of his mouth. Young Jimmy pushed with every ounce of his strength to shut the big door so the others couldn't escape.

I was tempted to stand my ground and take my chances that the boy could talk some sense into his dad. After all, this was my family lying up there in that loft, now completely at the mercy of this pitchfork-wielding madman. But what could one little pup do? Realizing the answer to that question was little or nothing, I put my head down, started running as fast as I could, and headed out onto the gravel road. I never looked back.

To this day, the lasting picture in my mind is of that farmer holding the pitchfork over Momma and my seven siblings. For the longest time after my

Houdini impersonation I woke up nights to that image. Eventually, I got to the point where I didn't wake up from my nightmares, but I never did get over the picture in my mind. No wonder I was never particularly fond of Grant Wood and his "American Gothic" painting.

Once out on the road, I had no idea what was in store for me, but I decided that, whatever it might be, it beat the alternative. I ran as far as my stubby legs could go, determined to put as much distance between me and the farm as possible. I just kept running, stopping once in a while only long enough to catch my breath. Not wanting to end up as roadkill, I tried to stay off the pavement but found it tough going in the snow-covered ditches. I was beginning to tire and wishing I had some of my momma's milk. After all, that was the only form of nourishment I had known up to this point. But I had to forget the past and decide what to do next.

With such short days in the dead of winter, dusk came early. With nightfall on the horizon, I needed to figure out some basics. How was I going to find anything to eat? And where would I sleep? It was pretty obvious to me that I was ill equipped to do much about either of these predicaments.

I had just stopped to ponder my next move when

I heard a car rumble up behind me. A black-and-white sedan with a red flashing bulb on the roof pulled over on the side of the road. Two uniformed officers slowly got out of the car, a short portly man on the driver's side and a slender, petite woman riding shotgun. Each adjusted their wide-brimmed hats as if they were primping for some beauty contest. They strode towards me, perfectly synchronized, step for step.

"Well, if he isn't the cutest little bugger you ever saw," said the woman.

"Does he have any tags on him, Barbara?" the man inquired.

Even though neither of them was holding a pitchfork I still didn't see this as a great position to be in, maybe because each had a pistol in a holster on one side and a club dangling from their other leg. With that thought I did a one-eighty and started to make my second escape of this already long day. But before I could get more than a few yards, the woman quickly caught up, grabbed me by the neck and turned to her partner. "No, Hank, I don't see any kind of ID on the little guy. Poor thing, he is shivering and whimpering for his momma. He must not be more than six weeks old."

"Well, we better get the dog over to the shelter

and let them deal with him."

"Oh, I know we should," Barbara said, "but I sure would like to take him home with me."

"You know the rules, Barbara. County Ordinance 23-F4-66 requires all stray animals to be surrendered immediately to the shelter."

Just my luck. I get picked up by this sweet, sympathetic woman and she has Hard-core Hank for a partner, acting like a big shot, citing ordinances and all. Even though she wore a uniform, Barbara had a gentle touch. I could easily see myself going home with her.

"Oh, I know the darn rules, Hank, but just look at those sorrowful little eyes," she said as she gently wiped my paws to remove the snow that had built up on them during my wanderings through the country ditches. I decided a little light whimpering might be the perfect complement to those sorrowful eyes I now had clearly fixed on Barbara's peepers.

"Suit yourself, Barbara, but don't expect me to come to your defense if the sheriff finds out you are harboring a runaway."

You would have thought Officer By-the-Book was referring to some guy in pin-striped pajamas on the lam from a maximum security prison rather than little old me.

"Well, okay, Hank, the last thing a rookie female cop needs is to be written up for harboring a criminal," Barbara said with equal doses of sarcasm and resignation in her voice.

After she was sure I stopped whimpering, Barbara carried me back to the squad car, opened the rear door, and gently sat me down on the seat. With a soft pat on the head, she tried to reassure me that all would be okay.

Old Henry had a bit different take on the matter. He slipped behind the steering wheel and reached around to close an imposing steel grate separating the front from the back seat. The whole thing was a bit preposterous. What did he think I was going to do? Did he think I was some 150-pound Rottweiler that was going to jump up to the front and attack one or both of them?

Off we went. I was surprised the guy didn't start his siren wailing as we cruised down the highway. Fortunately for my badly bruised psyche, we headed in the opposite direction from whence I had trotted just minutes earlier. After a short ride we pulled up in front of the shelter. My new best friend, Barbara, opened the back door and peeked in at me all huddled up in one corner of the backseat. "Come on, little fella, let's go inside and see if we can't get you cared for."

Seeing that I didn't have much choice in the matter, I let her scoop me in her arms and off we went into the stark-looking building. The place made me feel like I was at the booking station in the local precinct house. I kept waiting for somebody to take my paw prints.

"Who you got there, Barbara?" inquired a perky young girl working the front counter.

"Oh, hi, Judy. We found this little guy trotting down the highway just north of here. No tags, no form of ID whatsoever. He must be no more than six weeks old. He certainly seems frightened about something. I wanted to take him home but Hank insisted we play by the rules and bring him to you guys," she replied with a sparkle in her eye.

With that, Barbara gave me a gentle smooch on the snout and carefully handed me off to the shelter worker like a quarterback handing off the pigskin to a tailback lunging forward for a first down.

"Thanks for bringing him in, Barbara. We'll get him settled in and put out a notice. Maybe he just strayed from home and his owners will call us when they realize he is missing."

As the two officers turned to leave, I thought to myself that there were two chances of that happening:

slim or none. Although Sonny seemed genuinely distraught by my quick exit from the hayloft, I could only guess that Farmer Friday figured his overpopulation problem had just been reduced by one-eighth with my departure.

With me in her arms, Judy opened the door leading from the reception area to a back room. Immediately, a deafening chorus of howls greeted us. The room had the strangest layout you could imagine. I figured that the accommodations would be similar to what I had just left behind. You know, a giant bed of straw for all the strays waiting out their time at the shelter. On the contrary. The room consisted of one long concrete hallway with what seemed like an endless line of chain-link pens on both sides. The smell of the place reminded me of the hayloft, but with an anti-septic institutional odor thrown in for good measure.

As Judy hustled me down the hallway, the mournful howling grew even louder. From the safety of my newest best friend's arms I glanced from side to side to see who the other unlucky dogs were. Mostly mutts, as you might expect, with an occasional lab or retriever thrown into the mix, or more aptly, thrown in with the mixes. Most of the dogs came right up to the front doors of their pens to check out this pitiful little Terrier, although I noticed a few senior citizens content to view the proceedings from a horizontal position. Leave it to the younger ones to get up close and personal with this newcomer.

Towards the back of the hall a vacant pen appeared on the left side. Judy opened the door, carefully holding onto me with her free arm. Once we were both safely within the confines of the pen she gently laid me down on a bed of old blankets, a very suitable substitute for the straw I had grown accustomed to in the loft. After a pat on the head she stepped out of the pen and closed the door behind her. By this time the choir boys and girls seemed to have sung themselves out and only a few occasional whines broke the silence.

I had barely had a chance to check out my new surroundings when Judy returned with two bowls, one filled half full of milk and the other sprinkled with a handful of strange-looking peanut-sized brown nuggets.

"Not sure if you have even been weaned yet from your momma, little fella, so I brought you some warm milk and a bit of puppy chow. Take your pick."

It seemed like days since I had tasted Momma's milk. Still, with all that had happened, I wasn't in much of a mood to eat. Not wanting to seem ungrateful, I lapped a bit of the warm milk and plopped down on the blankets.

"Sleep tight, little guy. Tomorrow will be a better day, I promise."

With that, Judy stepped out of my pen and closed the door behind her. As the sound of her clicking heels echoed off the concrete floor, I closed my eyes and could only hope that she was right. I held onto the promise of a better day, one without any pitchforks, emergency exits from the second floor, blaring sirens, or uniformed officers.

I'm not sure. Is this what they mean by making a good first impression?

Four

FIRST IMPRESSIONS

Before long I settled into a relatively predictable routine at the shelter: two meals a day, regular walks with one of the volunteers, and so on. I had quickly learned to eat dog food and found it a reasonable substitute for my momma's milk. Still, I sorely missed seeing her and my seven little siblings. To make matters worse, I'd been at the shelter now for a few months and hadn't come close to finding a permanent home. Occasionally someone came down the hallway to check out all of us strays. Mostly they were gawkers, the kind who show up at realtors' open houses out of curiosity but with no intention of ever making an offer.

I was naturally eager to find a home, one as far away from that hay loft as possible. Maybe I was too eager? Maybe I needed to shower more often?

DUFFY

Should I consider an under-leg deodorant? Believe me—all sorts of crazy thoughts go through your mind when you are on the inside looking out.

On a dreary Saturday afternoon in the fall, I spent the morning listening to the rain drip from the eaves just outside my window. All of my compatriots were feeling a bit down on this gloomy day and there wasn't even the usual chatter amongst the gang. I curled up in the far corner of my pen, figuring an afternoon nap might be in order.

Just about the time I started to doze off, I heard Judy's voice and looked up to see her ever-cheery face in front of my pen. "Hey, Duff. There is a nice couple out front that wants to meet you."

I was just getting used to my new moniker. Judy had given me the name Duffy a few days after my arrival and she often shortened it to just Duff for what I took as a subtle indication of affection.

Oh, sure, more gawkers, I thought to myself.

Still, the thought that someone actually came just to meet me sounded encouraging. I slowly walked from the corner of my pen to meet Judy at the door, trying not to make the retriever mix in the next pen over feel any worse than he already did. He had been in the joint even longer than me. A twelve-year-old with a set of bad hips wasn't likely to find a new home anytime soon.

"Hey, buddy, maybe picking you as this week's 'Pet of the Week' wasn't such a bad idea," Judy said as she snapped a leash onto my collar and led me down the long hallway.

Come to find out, the couple had seen a mug shot of me in their local paper. Apparently what drew them in to take a look was that I indeed was "Pet of the Week." You have to understand that this was in the days before the Internet. People actually read their local rag and here was my likeness for the whole town to see.

Whether the people at the shelter were desperate to find me a home or if it was simply my handsome looks that resulted in this high honor I will never know. But it didn't really matter. Pet of the Week is Pet of the Week any way you slice it. And here were two people who had taken one look at that handsome dude in the newspaper and couldn't resist a visit to the shelter to check him out—even if the description underneath my mug shot labeled me as a "lively Bull Terrier."

Judy opened the door to the room where the couple waited. They both looked to be in their thirties, straight out of suburbia, both sporting blue jeans and running shoes. Most encouraging to me was the absence of any kids. Granted, beggars can't be choosers, but I really preferred to not share the limelight with any munchkins.

Whether or not I made a good first impression is hard to say. I suppose it depends on whom you are trying to impress. All you need to visualize to comprehend this initial encounter is a pinball machine. The poor unsuspecting couple served as the bumpers and, you guessed it, I was the pinball. Unlike Tommy, there was no need for a pinball wizard. I bounced off the walls of the dimly lit room of my own free will; that is, whenever I wasn't bouncing off one of them. Stopping long enough to lick one of them in the face, I raced to the far end of the room where I bounded off the wall and landed back in the other one's face. Now, I ask you, does this sound like the way to make a good first impression? My answer to my own question would be a resounding no. Still, I couldn't help myself. This couple had come just to see Yours Truly.

"Oh, he settles right down after a few minutes. He just likes to show off that personality of his," Judy tried to reassure the young couple as they took turns fielding me like a catcher bracing for a home-plate collision.

"Yes, he does seem to have quite the personality,

doesn't he!" the young woman piped in, catching her breath as I careened off the far wall and headed back for a run at her other half.

"It's just that when they have been here for a few months, as Duff has, there is a lot of pent-up energy and they need to work it off," Judy pleaded my case as best she could, given my theatrics.

Starting to feel a bit winded, I finally settled down long enough so the couple could give me a good looking over. A few pats on the head and a couple of dog biscuits later, I was feeling pretty good about the prospects. Judy explained that I was up to date on all my vaccinations and had received a good bill of health from the vet. Of course, I would need to be "fixed" as soon as I was adopted. Although it seemed a bit incongruous that a clean bill of health left anything to fix, I let that comment pass in the excitement of the moment.

Once I chilled out, the guy finally spoke up. "Well, he is adorable and we just love him. Still, this is a big step and we may need to think it over for a few days. See if we have someplace to keep the little guy. And there is a chance my wife is allergic to dogs, so we may want to talk to our doctor about that. We will try to let you know in a few days."

That was it. I had blown my chance at freedom.

My one opportunity to blow this pop stand and I had to act like some goofball out in public for the first time. See where they could keep me? Check out the wife's allergies? Pretty lame excuses if you ask me. As they each gave me one last pat on the head I figured that was the last I would ever see of the two of them. And I wasn't sure I could blame them. Judy led me back to my pen and I glanced over to the twelve-year-old retriever mix. He gave me that look that said, "Sorry, pal. Maybe next time."

Well, life is full of miracles and, after the one involving my birth, the next one I witnessed came just a few days after my pinball impersonation. I was still feeling sorry for myself, moping around my pen, when Judy suddenly appeared and very nonchalantly announced that there was some guy out front waiting to see me. Regardless of what they say about *old* dogs, I had no doubt about the ability to teach a *new* dog new tricks. I had seen the error of my ways. This time I strode out to the waiting area calmly, intent on putting my best paw forward.

"Hi, Duff. Good to see you again, fella. Are you ready to go home?"

Here he was again. One half of the twosome that I thought I had scared the poop out of just days before. Now he was calling me by my name. Not only that, he was asking me if I wanted to go *home*, an idea foreign to me up to this point in my life. My first reaction was to barrel into him with all my might. On second thought I gave a very modest "woof," a more civilized way to say that, absolutely, the lively Bull Terrier was ready to go home.

Five

QUERY, QUERY
(HEAVEN)

Every morning began with a light rain shower, each time adding luster to the perpetually emerald green grass. On cue, the rain tapered off to a mist-like spray, and in the distance the sun made its first appearance on another glorious day in paradise. The whole effect produced a rainbow containing every color of the universe.

I had just finished my morning meal and was lying frog-like, soaking in the radiant sun, when I spotted Rex trotting towards me. "Top of the morning to you, Duff," Rex chirped, joining the chorus of birds calling out from their perches in the blossoming trees.

"And to you, too, Rex. I was just enjoying a bit

of the morning sun before I set to work on my tale."
Whenever I saw Rex these days he was always anxious
to hear how my story was progressing, so I tried this
fine morning to cut him off at the pass. "I actually
have four chapters written and feel like I'm getting
up a full head of steam."

"Terrific, my boy. This would seem the perfect
time to get that query letter off."

"Sorry, Rex, but I thought we decided I would
write an entire book, not just a letter. And why would
I need to write a letter asking someone a bunch of
questions?" About the time I thought I had this
whole publishing business figured out, Rex would
blindside me with some confounding statement such
as this one about a query letter.

"Oh, no, Duff, you are indeed writing a book
and I want you to keep your head down and continue
working on your story. Allow me to explain the
nature of a query letter. Normally, you as the author
sends a letter to a list of agents, asking if they would
like to represent you. Once you strike an agreement
with one of them, the agent in turn submits the book
to a publisher. But since you already have an agent in
the form of Yours Truly, I will query some editors at
the big publishing houses to determine their interest
in the book. Along with my letter, I'll send off those

first four chapters you said you've written."

"That sounds great. But I do have something that has been bothering me since we first talked about my tale. I am curious how you intend to communicate with some two-legged editor back on planet Earth."

"Not a problem, old chap. The wonders of Heaven and Earth technology. I am sure you have heard of email, have you not? By using the Heavennet, I am able to interface with Earth's Internet and email my query letter to a handful of editors, attaching those first four chapters, and we wait to see who responds. At this point, why do any of them need to know the query is coming from a dog? And for that matter one emailing from *up here* rather than *down there*?" Rex explained, gesturing with that bullet head of his first up and then down as a reminder of where we now resided in relation to the rest of the universe.

"Sounds good, Rex. I will turn my attention back to my tale and leave you to work on your query letter," I responded, proud of myself for picking up some of the lingo.

"Go to it, Duff. And have a great day," my Terrier friend offered as he turned and trotted down the road as if on a mission from some higher power.

I did in fact have a great day and had made some more progress on my tale. The sun was just beginning to set as I looked up to see Rex approaching, a scrap of paper clenched tightly in his molars.

"Here 'tis, Duff," Rex chirped, dropping the paper in front of me. "Give it a quick read and let me know what you think. If it sounds good, I will send it off posthaste."

Not bothering with an explanation of what post-haste might entail, I anxiously turned to Rex's draft:

Dear Editor,

You have undoubtedly witnessed the recent popularity of dog books. Not since the days of Lassie and Rin Tin Tin have dogs been the hot property they are today. In reading your profile in the latest edition of Writer's Market, *I learned of your passion for dogs and animal rescue and thus my pitch for my client's riveting story,* Duff y: The Tale of a Terrier.

Duffy is no ordinary talking dog, but then what canine with the gift of gab would be considered normal? His adopted parents rescued him from a local shelter and for thirteen years he showed them unconditional love, but in all that time never said a word to them. It was only after he moved on to the afterlife that Duffy began to put his thoughts on paper, with the encouragement of his buddy, a literary easterner of the Boston Terrier persuasion named Rex. Under the tutelage of Rex, Duff learns about genres, what sells, and other nuances of the book trade.

Duff y: The Tale of a Terrier *has its genesis in the stories*

QUERY, QUERY (HEAVEN)

of Duff's time as an only dog. Knowing the grief that his human parents must be feeling upon his passing, Duffy resolves to write a story to help ease their pain. Attached are the first four chapters of what will ultimately be a 45,000-word first-dog account of this Terrier's time as a terra or earth dog.

Tongue now out of my cheek, I present my client's credentials. First, he is well versed in the inner workings of shelter life, having spent a good deal of time working at a facility much like the one where Duffy had been placed for adoption. Second, my client has extensive formal training, earning both basic and advanced degrees in dog obedience. I trust the attached chapters will give you a keen sense for his familiarity with the canine world. Having spent much of my own adult life reading tales from the animal world, I had an eerie feeling that I was reading prose crafted from the paw of a four-legged creature rather than some two-legged surrogate.

Thank you for your consideration. I look forward to hearing from you soon and sharing more of Duffy's tale.

Regards,

R. Terrence Bostwick III

rtbostwick3@hvmail.com

I turned to Rex and tried to choose my words carefully. Given our growing friendship and knowing of his unabashed enthusiasm for my tale, I didn't want to sound the least bit ungrateful. But still I had some questions.

"This sounds great, Rex. Your query has a very convincing tone to it and, if I were an editor, I would certainly want to take a closer look. But once your tongue is out of your cheek you make it sound as if this tale is being written by a human, rather than by me. Is that above board?"

"Duff, Duff. Surely you can understand my position in this matter. Here we are, two dogs no longer connected to planet Earth and I am to tell some editor that the tale is in fact written by a dog, and oh, by the way, the canine author now resides in Heaven? Do you know how far that would get us, old boy?"

"I suppose you are right, Rex. It's just that I don't believe in stretching the truth. So we go along for now with the facade that this tale is being written by some human. But the credentials? Well versed in the inner workings of shelter life? Extensive formal training with basic and advanced degrees in obedience training?"

"But, Duff, did you not tell me that you spent eight long months in a shelter, and would this not qualify *you* as an expert in the inner workings of this life? And did you not also tell me that it was *you* in fact who went through two different obedience classes? So we stretch the truth a bit for the time being about who this story is actually written by, you or your human alter ego. But, hey, the other two statements—regarding *your* credentials—these are certifiably accurate. In my estimation, two of three isn't so bad, wouldn't you say? If need be, we can always, at a later point, clear up this minor annoyance about who actually wrote the story."

My head was spinning, trying its best to sort through the inestimable logic being espoused by Rex the wonder dog. A complete understanding of his explanation would have to wait for another day. "Fair enough, Rex, but I do have one last question. R. Terrence Bostwick III?"

"Oh, that. That's *my* pseudonym!"

"Your soo-da-what!" I exclaimed in another one of my occasional fits of bewilderment at hearing something strange pass from Rex's mouth.

"My pseudonym. It means my pen name. It is a fictitious name often used by those in literary circles. It allows me to remain anonymous, which is not such a bad idea for a dog trying to make it as an agent. I hope you like it. I dreamed it up myself. The R. is short for Rex, Terrence a reference to my Terrier disposition, and Bostwick in deference to my proper Bostonian roots. And being a third never hurts when you are dealing with the upper crust of the intellectual, scholarly crowd."

I have to say that I found Rex's ways both exasperating and exhilarating—at the same time. But I also had no doubt that R. Terrence Bostwick III didn't just fall off the turnip truck. The guy knew his stuff.

Now that is one bad haircut!

Six

PERSONAL HYGIENE

Late September. Ah, the fresh, crisp autumn air. The smell of leaves burning somewhere off in the distance. Birds chirping in the trees. Trees just starting to turn colors. My senses were alive as I proudly strode out the door of the shelter with my new dad. What a great day to be alive. The hayloft was but a fading memory.

"Hop up, Duff," Dad instructed as he lifted the gate on the back end of a vehicle that looked much different from the only other mode of transportation I had experienced in my young life, that dreadful cop car. Turns out this was one of those SUVs. Eager to show I could follow instructions, I hopped up into the back.

Once comfortably seated I realized why these were called SUVs. It was obviously short for "Sit Up Vertically," which was exactly what I could do in the back of this amazing rig. This vehicle was tailor-made for a dog. As Dad closed the hatch behind me I realized that I could sit on my back haunches and very comfortably look out either side window or the back and survey the entire landscape spread out before me. What a delight! *Sure beats being plopped down on the backseat of a cop car*, I thought to myself as we cruised down the highway. *Yeah, these SUVs were the only way to travel.*

Thinking we were headed to my new home, I was surprised when, after a few minutes of pleasant driving through the countryside, we pulled up in front of a place that didn't resemble a house. Nor a shelter or a farm for that matter, the two other types of housing I had some familiarity with during my brief life. A poodle was just marching out the door with his master in tow. Although the dog was grinning from ear to ear, his haircut looked like something out of a bad dream. The guy was shaved down to his birthday suit over much of his body with little balls of fur left standing in other places, most conspicuously on the top of his head and his rear end. If the bad haircut wasn't humiliation enough, the poor boy sported a big, red bow tied around his neck. Still, he strode out of the building as if he had just been called up to receive an Oscar.

Knowing full well that this sort of shame and

humiliation couldn't be heaped on me—after all, I was a short-hair—I hopped right down when Dad opened the back of the Sit Up Vertically. He suggested I relieve myself prior to stepping inside, so I marked an especially fragrant bush off to the side of the building. Once inside, a chipper young lady behind the counter greeted us. "Welcome, sir, to Sandy's Snip, Clip, Fluff and Buff. How can we help you and your little companion today?"

Dad proudly introduced his new pride and joy to Sandy. "Good morning. This here is Duffy and he just came from the shelter so he needs a good bath. He is pretty much a wash-and-wear dog, so no need for a haircut, just a good thorough bathing."

"Sounds good. We'll give the little guy a good going over, clip the nails, check the glands. He should be good to go in a couple of hours."

Of course, I had never had a bath before, at least not one administered by some human. And what is this about checking the glands? Anything like checking the oil on that SUV?

My first introduction to personal hygiene came from my birth mother, who licked all of us pups during those first few weeks in the hayloft. During my time at the shelter I had picked up on the habit, giving myself a daily licking, thinking this was all I ever needed. After all, it wasn't like I was out rolling around in roadkill every day there at the shelter.

"You be a good boy, Duff," Dad said as he carefully handed me over to Sandy. I could tell by the look in his eyes that he wasn't too keen on leaving me for any longer than necessary. After all, we had been together less than an hour at this point.

The fluff and buff went surprisingly well. Sure, I hadn't rolled around in roadkill but, after a few months in the shelter, my coat didn't have quite the natural shine it did when I first arrived there. And I was beginning to itch. As ambidextrous as a dog is, there remain certain critical spots you just can't reach. Sandy worked some shampoo into my coat. As she gently massaged the muscles in my back I was beginning to see how the other half lived. So relaxing. I could take this for a long time.

After a few minutes of heavenly bliss, Sandy rinsed me off with warm water. Thinking I could take it from here, I gave myself a thorough shaking, the kind only a dog can do. But I was far from dry. Sandy reached over to a shelf and grabbed a peculiar-looking device. It looked like a bloated version of those guns that the two cops dangled from their legs that fateful day they brought me to the shelter. Naturally, I was a bit apprehensive when Sandy aimed this thing at me and flipped a switch on the side of it. Soon I realized I had nothing to worry about. As she directed the dryer at me I felt a warmth, like I was lying out in the sun on a summer's day.

I will spare you the details of the gland checking. Let's just say that it didn't involve a dipstick but rather the nice lady's thumb and forefinger squeezed against a strategic spot on my posterior. Not the most pleasant sensation in the world but, after falling into such a state of bliss from my fluff and buff, I barely objected to this minor invasion of my privacy.

Once this bit of diagnostic work was done, Sandy led me back to a small pen, not unlike my accommodations at the kennel. I was so relaxed that I nodded off almost immediately. I barely heard her voice when she later roused me and said it was time to go home. As Sandy led me out to the front room, there stood Dad, grinning from ear to ear, and going on and on about what a handsome dude I was.

Yes, it was time to go home.

**Curiosity may have done in the cat,
but not so for a dog.**

Seven
HOUSE AND HOME

Not to get too philosophical—after all, I was a Terrier, not a French Poodle—but what *is* the difference between a house and a home? A house is where you sleep, which for us canines is pretty darn important since we spend about twenty hours a day in a reclining position. A house provides that proverbial roof over your head, whereas a home is something entirely different.

You see, after having spent so much time in the shelter, I was desperately looking for a home. Sure, the basics of life, including a roof over one's head, are pretty important. But I needed to find a home and a family that would take me in and call me their own. Given my long stay at the shelter I had my doubts that this would ever happen. But from that first day when I left the shelter, it quickly became clear that these two people who adopted me intended to give me a home—and it sure wasn't going to be one where the buffalo roam.

I found out fairly soon that my new folks could be a bit neurotic at times. For instance, they felt they had to make a decision on where I would sleep, even *before* they brought me to my new home. Supposedly, this accounted for their reluctance to take me home after our initial meeting. They needed to think things through. For starters, would I be housed inside or outside? Had they asked, I certainly would have barked my opinion for the former. Don't get me wrong. I loved the great outdoors as much as the next dog, but does sleeping out under the stars night after night sound like the way a civilized dog should go through life? I think not.

When Dad brought me home on that life-changing day, it was not clear what the two of them had in mind. The house we pulled up in front of looked very nice. The essence of suburbia. A two-story frame structure with cute little shutters, a chimney, a front porch, and a two-car garage. The house had a roof over it and that is what mattered most to me.

I had heard some of the dogs at the shelter talk about how they were looking forward to sleeping in the bed with their masters once they found homes. I just assumed I would be doing the same. I felt like I had arrived, a roof over my head and a bed to sleep in.

Turns out, that wasn't *exactly* what the folks had in mind for me. In fact, I wasn't at all sure *what* they had in mind for me. As soon as Dad and I pulled in the drive, Mom came running out the front door to greet us. "Welcome home, Duff. We can't wait to show you your new digs."

Mom gave me a gentle pat on the head as Dad handed her my leash and she led me around to the rear of the house. Dad opened a gate and Mom let me loose in the fenced-in backyard. After a few quick sprints to get the lay of the land, I noticed this strange-looking structure on the deck and sauntered over to check it out. It was rectangular in design, about three feet tall, made out of wood, with a small opening at one end. The best way I can describe it is that the thing looked like a miniature barn, complete with a hip roof with little red shingles.

Naturally, my first reaction to this clever architectural feat was not a very positive one. I swear it was an exact replica of the barn I had come into the world in and narrowly escaped from only a few months earlier. I mean the darn thing was cute, but certain images will forever be stuck in my mind and this was one of them. The folks were eager for me to see the inside of this structure.

"Go ahead, buddy, check it out," Dad gently nudged me towards a small opening in the front of it. Little did he know that I expected to look in and see a farmer glaring back at me, pitchfork in hand.

Not wanting to seem ungrateful, I finally summoned the courage to take a peek inside. I cautiously stuck my nose in the small opening. The inside of this mini-barn was pretty sparse, although it was covered with a nice layer of straw. Still, it felt a bit claustrophobic in there. I stayed inside just long enough to give the sense of being impressed and then popped back out.

"Isn't it great, Duff?" Dad offered, doing his best to sell me on this strange contraption. I gave a woof and followed my folks into the house for the first time.

Once inside they led me over to an equally strange-looking contraption in the kitchen. It also stood about three feet high, but unlike the miniature barn this thing was made out of wire and you could see right through it. Like the little barn outside, it also had an opening at one end. Curiosity may have killed the cat, but I had never heard of it having that effect on a dog; so for the second time in a matter of minutes I ventured through another small cavity. No straw this time, but a very comfortable blanket spread out over a Styrofoam mat that covered the bottom of this peculiar apparatus. And the added bonus of being able to keep an eye out from inside this engineering marvel.

The rest of the day proved quite relaxing: time in the backyard playing catch with Dad, watching Mom prepare the evening meal, me eating my first chow in my new house. When it came time for "bed" that first night, I positioned myself by the stairs leading to the second floor, assuming that was probably where we would all sleep. The folks saw me sitting by the steps with a somewhat forlorn look on my face.

"Oh, look, hon, Duff thinks he is going to be sleeping upstairs with us," Mom said to Dad as she led me back in the general direction of the kitchen and the wire apparatus I had been introduced to earlier in the day. Dad opened the door and Mom gently coaxed me in. Having not been born yesterday, but rather a few months back, it was clear to me that this was where I would be spending the night, sawing my first logs in my new digs.

At first I tried to act a bit offended that I wasn't being invited upstairs. But then I started thinking a bit more logically. Let's see now. This structure is about three feet high with an opening leading into a cushioned mat covered with a blanket. Just outside on the deck is a similar apparatus, about the same height, with an opening about the same size, and with some straw that could serve as a blanket. Already late September, there was a chill in the autumn air. Okay, fair enough. I got the picture and shuffled into the structure that from that first night in my new home until the very last would be my house.

As I learned later, the rectangular mini-barn out on the deck was called a dog house. I thought a dog house was where humans go when they do something really stupid, but come to find out that was just another of those silly expressions humans use. This cute little barn with the red shingles was the genuine article, an authentic dog house. Over the years I came to like my dog house. It was a great place to lounge while keeping an eye on the neighbor's cat. On a warm summer day I could lay inside in the cool shade of the dog house and stick my head out just far enough to soak in the sun's rays. But still, I much preferred my inside "house" to spend the night.

The folks had a name for my inside house. They called it my crate. They cringed whenever friends referred to it as a cage, like the folks were harboring some wild beast in it. I know, just semantics, but these sorts of things were important to them. My crate was the darndest thing. When we went on the road—which we often did over the years we spent together—my crate folded up like a suitcase and went with us. Now let me ask. How many humans can say that when they travel they are able to take their house with them?

I will never forget that first morning at home. The sun was just coming up as I awoke from a great night's rest in my new digs. I heard footsteps from the stairs and pretty soon I saw the two of them bounding down to greet me. What happened next you may not believe, but I would swear on a stack of Bibles to this. It really did happen. Very slowly and cautiously Mom opened the crate door. Dad knelt down in front of the opening and reached in and grabbed me around my belly, like he was reaching into the refrigerator at the grocery store to retrieve a gallon of milk. Before I could protest I was whisked out of the crate and carried like a sack of potatoes out the back door.

As soon as I was outside, I glanced back with a puzzled look on my face. The two of them started encouraging me to "do my business." It took me a minute but I figured it out. They didn't trust me to wait until I was outside to take a tinkle, and so they were going to insure that I peed outside and not inside. How? By unceremoniously carrying me out the back door. For Heaven's sake, did they think I was born in a barn? Sorry, wrong expression, since as you know, I was in fact born in a barn. But you get the picture. What were they thinking anyway? Suffice it to say that they soon learned to trust me and it wasn't long before I was allowed to maintain my dignity and walk outside on my own to "do my business" and start the day.

There you have it. As it turned out, I had multiple houses and one home. I had the house that I shared with my folks and in that house I had my own house, the aforementioned crate. My traveling house, as it were. And I had my cute little dog house out on the deck. But do you know what? From all of this, from that first day forward, I only had one home.

Over my lifetime we lived in a number of different houses. But there was only one home I ever had. You see, home was wherever I was with my folks. That could be in their house, it could be out on the road on one of our adventures. Where we were never mattered to me. As long as I could wake up in the morning and see my adoring folks, I knew I was home.

I just assumed altering a dog was similar
to the work of a tailor. You know, let the
waistband out a couple inches.

Eight
NEUTERHOOD

I had only been at my new house and home a few weeks. The day started out like many others: out for a brisk jog with the folks, and the opportunity to sniff all of the wonderful aromas along our route, and back home for a hearty breakfast. Just about the time I was ready to curl up for a morning nap—I highly recommend a good nap after every meal, it doesn't need to be long, just enough to recharge the batteries—the call came from Dad.

"Load up, Duff, we're going for a ride."

What he failed to tell me was that this particular ride would end in one of the most life-altering—not to mention physically altering—experiences I would ever have.

Before I had time to get settled into the back of the Sit Up Vertically, I see we are pulling into the vet's office. Nothing wrong with that, right? Probably just check my weight and give me a quick inspection. You know, like when you buy a new car and you take it back after driving it a week to make sure everything is working as it should. There would probably be the standard praise from the vet about my tip-top shape and rugged good looks. Then it would end with a pat on the head from the vet and a pet tab for being a nice boy.

Yeah, well, think again. Next thing I know, the vet's assistant is leading me down the hallway. Still, it couldn't be too bad. I turn in time to see Mom and Dad smiling and giving me a wink to assure me that they will see me soon.

Once propped up on a table in the back room, the vet sticks a rubber band around my front left leg, pulls out a needle, and jabs it into a spot just above where he had wrapped the rubber band. Within a few minutes I start to feel pretty woozy and, before I know what hits me, I am out like a light. Zonked. Off in slumberland. Sweet dreams for this puppy.

When I awoke, I felt a bit stiff and it took a couple of minutes to recall where I was when I last had all my senses about me. This surely wasn't home. The sterile, antiseptic feel of the place was a quick reminder that I was in the vet's office. I felt especially sore around the old private parts—although as we all well know they aren't that terribly private on a dog!

It didn't take long to realize something, or, more accurately, some things were missing. A quick inventory confirmed that two of those very distinctive male private parts were unaccounted for—missing in action as it were—except it would appear that I slept through all of the action. Where those parts normally resided was instead a fancy row of stitching—and we're not talking about the type around my nose, either.

Outrage is probably the best description for my initial reaction to this shocking discovery on my part. I willingly hop in the car for a leisurely ride and the next thing you know I have been altered. Not just inconvenienced. Not just put upon. We're talking altered. Remember that "Pet of the Week" description of me as a "lively Bull Terrier?" Well, now, it needed another adjective to be totally accurate: "*altered* lively Bull Terrier." And I will tell you what. I wasn't feeling terribly lively, either.

I mean, who would be happy to wake up one morning, look down, and realize that you had entered a whole new category in life? Crazy thoughts start running through your head. Will I need to have my city license changed, now that I have changed? Next time I enter a 10K companion animal road race will there be an appropriate box to check off since "male" just doesn't seem appropriate anymore? And what about the resume? How do I list my personal data, now that I have been *revised*?

Before I had a chance to steam over this outrageous turn of events for much longer, the owners show up all cheery. "How did our little man do?" Mom inquired of the vet.

"Duff was a real trooper," the guy in the white smock retorted. "He took it like a real man."

Yeah, and from what I can tell, it was to be the last thing I would take as a man. As we leave, the vet lays out all of the ground rules. "Just limit his activity for the next couple of days. No food until tomorrow morning, just keep his water bowl filled."

Forget the activity. The only pursuit I cared about at this point was inhaling a good meal. The way I had been treated, I should have been taken out immediately for a Kansas City rib eye. Instead they are being instructed to drive me home and fill up the old water bowl. Live it up, boy, have another swig of that good old H_2O!

Looking back, I am pretty certain the folks knew at the time how disgusted I was with this turn of events. What in the world were they thinking? They freely offered to anyone within earshot that I was about the most handsome guy on four legs they had ever seen. So why the shabby treatment? Why the humiliation that comes from realizing you are not half the man—or, to be more precise for the mathematically inclined, just a third of the man—you used to be?

In the short time I had been with them, what had I done to deserve such treatment? Did it ever enter their minds that someday I might want to start a family of my own? After all, I was just a youngster at that point. I had places to go, dogs to see, and, most importantly, wild oats to sew. Not only would the latter be a physical impossibility from here on out, I doubted many pooches of the opposite sex would be too attracted to a guy who no longer was even sure he should refer to himself as a guy.

Although I felt at the time like the most unique dog on the planet—a distinction in this case that wasn't terribly appealing to me—I later found out that this was the fate for many males of my species. I had suddenly entered the canine world of neuterhood. I had only recently ventured into puppyhood and now I had this to add to it. Better yet, to subtract from it. Forget adulthood. Don't even think about fatherhood anymore. This was totally out of the question.

I had heard about a procedure with the same desired effect that they sometimes do on males of the human species. Some long-winded medical term that started with a "V." From what I understood this type of procedure at least left the door open for a change of heart, a reversal down the road. Looking down to where those stitches now resided, I didn't see a whole lot of promise for any reversal in my case.

Let's just say that I stayed pretty steamed for some time after this life-altering experience. Oh, sure, I chomped down my meals as soon as they started feeding me again, and I willingly accepted the rawhides and pig's feet tossed my direction. But I certainly didn't indulge in any face-licking or snuggling up in front of the TV. I could pout with the best of them.

Just about the time I was starting to feel better, I was invited to hop in the Sit Up Vertically for another ride. Still feeling a bit sore down there, I needed a boost from Dad. I figured they were probably taking me to the pet store where I would be bribed with a humongous treat and the chance to pick out any toy I want. I would play it for all it was worth. Well, you can only imagine the look on my face when we pull into—you guessed it—the vet's office. The scene of the crime. The place where I lost my manhood and entered neuterhood. What more could they extract from me? What further insults could they heap upon me?

By now I am sweating bullets in anticipation of how those questions might be answered in the foreseeable future. I reluctantly follow the folks into the vet's office. A perky young assistant leads the three of us into the examining room. The kind of room that humans sit in reading a favorite magazine, waiting for the doctor to grace them with an appearance. The folks have a seat, but I prefer to stand. Boredom soon sets in. I mean really, how many times can you read the chart on the wall about the different breeds of canine, or gaze at the grotesque picture of what happens to a dog's mouth when the teeth aren't properly cared for? The name alone sounds disgusting—gingivitis.

About the time I was ready to make a break for the door like one of those villains in a cheap western movie, in walks the vet with a pair of scissors in his right hand. Is what I am seeing about to unfold before me even remotely possible? Because I took the last procedure like a man, they figure they won't even bother with a shot this time? My folks are going to hold me down and the vet in one clean sweep of those scissors will take the remaining bit of evidence that I was once a proud male? What kind of cruel joke is this anyway?

DUFFY

You can only imagine my relief when the vet reaches down and starts removing his fancy needlepoint from my belly. He seemed quite proud of his sew job and made some joke about how he missed his calling and what a terrific tailor he would have been. The folks felt compelled to go along and soon all three are yukking it up at my expense. *Glad I could accommodate them and provide a cheap bit of entertainment*, I thought to myself.

Although this latest bit of picking around was over in a matter of minutes, it sure seemed worth more than the measly pet tab tossed my way as I was lifted off the table. I certainly didn't refuse the peace offering. Still, I trotted out with a fairly indignant look on my face.

Life around the house pretty much returned to normal, as much as could be expected given what I had gone through. I continued to pout and sulk in the presence of the folks, just to let them know that I certainly didn't approve of this sort of treatment.

Shortly after this latest death march to the vet, the three of us made one of our occasional visits to the shelter. The folks liked to take me there and brag about what a wonderful member of the family I had become. I never minded going back for a visit, just as long as they didn't get any ideas about leaving me.

But what I saw that day as I hopped out of the Sit Up Vertically was deeply disturbing.

The scene unfolding before me was as fresh in my memory as if it had happened to me only days before. In fact, it had been a few months back since I had been picked up wandering the countryside and plopped down at the front desk of this same shelter. Now, here was a young Beagle mix—certainly not a Terrier, but handsome in his own right—being led into the shelter by a uniformed officer.

Once we had gone inside, the woman behind the desk shrugged her shoulders and said what a shame it was that this steady parade through their doors had to continue. If only owners would be more responsible and have their pets spayed or neutered. Well, given my recent experience, you can believe the mere mention of any variation on the word neuter was bound to get my attention. Be it a verb, a noun, past tense, future tense, it didn't matter. I was all ears.

She went on to explain how the huge problem of overpopulation of pets could be vastly reduced by spaying and neutering. Simple matter of mathematics, she said. Far too many abandoned and surrendered animals and too few shelters to look after them. And the problem only gets worse—in fact it multiplies, she said—when we canines multiply.

The example she gave was enough to make anyone sit up and take notice and not even expect a treat for sitting up. In a mere six years, one female dog and her offspring are capable of producing over 60,000 dogs. Was she telling me that without my little outpatient surgery I could have contributed to that many new little Duffs running the streets? As cute as we all know they would have been, that was beside the point. Who would care for them? Where would the food come from to feed 60,000 more mouths? And what would happen to them when there weren't enough families out there to adopt them all? This was a fate I certainly didn't want to think about.

Come to find out, my folks didn't have a choice in the matter. One of the conditions of my adoption was that I would be neutered immediately. No questions asked. No ifs, ands, or buts.

As the three of us walked out the door that day, I turned just in time to see the young Beagle mix being led down the hallway to the kennels. The paperwork had been processed and now the long wait would begin for the little guy. It was all I could do to watch as the volunteer did her best to convince the young lad that all was going to be okay. The pooch appeared timid and frightened and uncertain of what his fate might be on the other side of that door. I remembered the feeling all too well.

Once home, the folks asked if I would like to take a walk around the block before heading in for supper. I answered them in the only way that seemed appropriate at that moment. I jumped up and gave each of them a big old lick on the face as a way of saying, "Thanks for saving me and doing the right thing."

Who was I kidding with those crazy ideas of starting my own family? Sure, I was adopted. But with these two adoring parents standing there in the driveway admiring me that day, I knew I had all of the family I would ever need.

**I was perfectly happy as an only dog,
a litter of one, if you will.**

Nine

ONLY DOG

Yes, I had all of the family I would ever need. Humility aside for a minute, the fact was: my folks were crazy about me. My very own dog house surrounded by a fenced-in yard. My own bed inside the human house. Two squares a day and a steady diet of dog biscuits and rawhides thrown in for good measure. Daily walks and runs and on the weekends rides around town in the Sit Up Vertically. It was hard for me to imagine how life could be much better.

Still, when you have the kind of start in life I did, you are prone to occasional bouts of melancholy and worry. What if *I* was just the beginning? What if the folks planned to adopt more pets and, heaven forbid, what if that included a cat? And, what if down the road, their plans included the type of kids that crawl around, spit up, and eventually assume an upright position on two legs and learn to kick a soccer ball?

Well, over time it became clear that cats were not in the picture. When we were out walking I noticed the folks never paid much attention to Garfield's kind. Understand, they wouldn't let me off the leash to go chasing after one of the furballs, but it was obvious these animals of the feline persuasion didn't interest them the way we canines did. Dogs were another story. You never saw two people so infatuated by dogs. Big ones. Little ones. Short ones. Tall ones. Short hairs. Long hairs. Didn't matter, they were in love with dogs. On the one hand, I took great comfort in this knowledge. But down the road might they want to add to their canine collection?

As time went by, my fears proved unfounded. Sure, the folks cooed over every dog we encountered on our walks, but I eventually came to the realization that they were happy to view these others from a distance and be content spoiling Yours Truly.

Still, I had to wonder when the time might come to start a family. I had seen Dad a time or two stepping out of the shower and it was clear to me that he was what in the dog world would be called an "intact male." Obviously he hadn't shared the same fate as I had, the one I chronicled in the last chapter. And, the folks were both still relatively young and in the best of health. Okay, Dad was no spring chicken, pushing forty, but Mom was five years younger and she would be the one bearing the children. So why wouldn't the folks be planning to have their own litter sometime down the road? It seemed the American way.

Planning to have their own litter? Looking back, it is embarrassing to admit to my utter naïveté on the subject of human offspring. But, hey, what do you expect from some guy born in a barn? For all I knew it would be just like with dogs. Mom would deliver a litter and overnight there would be six or eight more mouths to feed. Looking back, how stupid on my part. While on the rare occasion some woman might deliver twins, triplets, or even quadruplets, this was pretty unusual.

I eventually came to understand that, in the absence of fertility drugs, most often there would be just one in a human litter, which of course doesn't make for much of a litter if you ask me. Still, the thought of even a single baby honing in on my territory didn't appeal to me. All I could do was wait it out and do my best to convince the folks that three was company, and four was a crowd.

So wait it out I did. To my everlasting delight, in all our years together, there was never any talk about additions to our family. None. No pitter patter of little feet, either two or four at a time. The folks seemed content to share their lives with just me.

Yes, I was to be an only dog. And happy for it.

I am fine with all the pomp;
it's just the circumstances
that concern me.

Ten

DUFFY PORTER, B.S., M.B.A.

I suppose it was to be expected. Both Mom and Dad were highly educated people, so it was only natural that they would want Number One And Only Son to be a learned pooch. Only the finest schools would do for their kid. Give him a chance to make it in the world. They believed in the value of an educated society and figured that extended to those of us walking around on four legs instead of two.

While Mom had a successful career in sales with a major corporation, Dad made higher education his livelihood. He taught at the university in something having to do with numbers. I never was certain what it was, but friends teased him about being a bean counter. He never seemed to mind and in fact took great pride in working with the future number-crunchers of the world.

Ironically, the fact that Dad was a teacher had something to do with my extensive training, as I will explain in more detail later. Shortly after entering neuterhood, the folks decided it was time to enroll me in an obedience class. I never cared much for the adjective "obedience" and always considered this a silly way to refer to a class full of dogs. Okay, so it signified the starting point in one's formal training. So why is it kindergarten and not Obedience Training for Five-year-olds when young Jimmy goes off for the first time?

But, as is my predisposition, I digress again. Because Dad was teaching on the only night I could start my obedience training, it was just Mom and me that set off for my first class. Sure I would have rather had both of them tag along. What young Terrier wouldn't want to avoid getting hit with the label "Momma's Boy" if he could? But I also understood that Dad had to do his part to help put food on the floor for me. So off I went to my first class, dragging Mom along behind me. However, as I was to quickly discover, dragging Mom along behind me wouldn't last long. That wasn't how obedient, well-trained dogs conducted themselves.

As we entered the classroom, it was a chaotic scene, to say the least. About a dozen other dogs were dragging their owners around the room in a state of frenzy. All the dogs acted as if they were entered in a contest to see who could bark the loudest, a million dog biscuits as the grand prize. As males will do, the guys were running from one pup to the next to check out the plumbing on each of their new classmates. I know. Not something those of the two-legged variety normally would do, but a very common habit among canines. The equivalent to shaking hands when humans meet someone new.

The chaos was short-lived. Out of nowhere he stepped into the room. I don't think any of us saw where he came from. He just sort of appeared, but the instant he did you knew he was there. He stood about six-foot-five and I'm guessing tipped the scales at around 245. He had a flat-top haircut and not a single whisker on his freshly shaven face. Not an ounce of fat on him. He was dressed in a pair of perfectly pressed Levis and a tight-fitting white T-shirt that served to accent his enormous biceps. The T-shirt was a walking advertisement for his business. Across the front it said Bob's Canine College. On the back in six-inch-high black lettering was the simple directive: "YOU **WILL** LEARN TO HEEL!"

Ever see that TV show about the hayseed country boy who went off to the Marine Corps? Remember the drill sergeant who tried to whip him into shape? Bob was a spitting image of the zealous sergeant and, as I studied the stern look on his face, I suddenly felt like that hayseed country boy.

To make things even scarier, Bob had a partner. The partner was on all four legs like all of us students and answered to the name Bub. A training prop, if you will. A visual study aid. Some teachers get their point across with a PowerPoint presentation and a laser pointer. Bob had Bub. Bub was the sleekest-looking specimen I had ever seen, and he carried himself with an air of confidence lacking in all of us rookies. Also, unlike myself and most of the others, Bub was a purebred, a Doberman Pinscher. He looked like he would just as soon take your head off as lick you in the face. You sure didn't see him going around sniffing the rear end of every other dog in the room.

BOB and BUB. Nothing fancy about the two of them. One syllable names. Didn't matter whether you read left to right or right to left. Take your pick. Their names came out the same either way. Humans have one of those nonsensical names for this, some-thing silly called a palindrome. But no nonsense about this pair. Both Bob and Bub had that same look in their eyes that said, "We are here to make your lives miserable."

With a bark to come to attention—the bark was from Bob, not Bub—the entire room turned quiet. Yes, you could have heard the proverbial pin drop. The first order of business was a roll call. I felt that it might help to break the ice to bark back to Bob when I heard my name called, but thought better of it and let Mom respond.

Bob explained to the class that he was in fact here to make our lives miserable, just as I suspected. But he quickly added that if we survived this six-week-long boot camp we would come out ready to tackle anything and everything life might throw at us. He said he realized that many of us had a rough start and that he was here to set us on the straight and narrow. The whole time Bob talked, Bub sat at perfect attention at Bob's side and never moved a hair on his body. If I hadn't seen him enter the room earlier, I would have sworn that Bub was one of those lawn ornaments someone might put in their yard to keep away the deer and rabbits.

After the roll call and introductory remarks, Bob reached into his Levis and pulled out a silver chain about six inches long. Each end of the chain had an extra-wide link on it. Bob demonstrated how to loop the chain through one end to create a collar.

Once the collar was in place he slipped it on Bub, the canine statuary continuing to sit perfectly still at his side.

As if he didn't already have our undivided attention, Bob explained with a twinkle in his eye that this particular device was called a choke collar. If the collar was put on correctly, all the handler needed to do was give a quick snap of the wrist and Fido would respond in the appropriate manner. It didn't take me long to understand that Mom was the handler and Yours Truly was Fido in this scenario. And while I certainly understood the premise behind this device, did Bob have to refer to it as a "choke collar"? Why not "attention getter"? Any name would be better than one that implied what might happen to you if you didn't mind your Ps and Qs. Though I quickly learned to pay attention when wearing my choke collar, I never did feel comfortable with the name.

Just as the back of Bob's T-shirt promised, we did learn to heel. In fact, that was the first order of business. Round and round we went in circles, first clockwise and then counterclockwise, heeling to our heart's content, and to the obvious pleasure of our "handlers."

Early on, we all learned that there were two primary forms of communication with your handler:

praise and correction. The first was a verbal form of feedback and was often accompanied by a nibble from the master's pocket. All you needed to hear were those magic words "goooood puppy" or some variation on this general theme, and you could be pretty certain you were in for a treat. A correction is what you did not want. Unlike praise, this form of communication was *not* verbal. Instead, it involved a quick snap on the old attention getter—again, I prefer this to choke collar—and we quickly got the message. One good correction and I listened up and stopped gawking at the cute Fifi on the other side of the ring.

This is probably as good a place as any to bring up what could be a highly embarrassing situation. Bob explained that any responsible owner would make sure that Fido be given the opportunity to "take care of business" before entering the classroom. But as we all well know, the adjective "responsible" isn't one that is always appropriate before the noun "owner." And even so, there were bound to be those jitters that some young pups experience the first night in the classroom. So Bob made it clear that it was mandatory for all owners to carry a baggie just in case. To demonstrate the technique he pulled a few kibbles from his pocket as a substitute for the genuine article.

He dropped them on the floor in front of him and then showed how to very efficiently snatch them up in one quick motion with a baggie and transfer them to the garbage can positioned at the far end of the room. It was all I could do to not look over at the pup sitting next to me and start giggling, but one look back at Bob and I realized that would be a big mistake.

Like any school with standards to uphold, we were given a homework assignment. Before next week's class we were to practice sitting and heeling, those basic skills learned the first night. Mom and Dad worked with me diligently, back and forth we went in our cul de sac, lest either they or I should incur the wrath of Bob and Bub.

Each successive week of class, something new was added. To start the second night's class, it was the "sit, stay." Bob demonstrated this basic technique with Bub. Bub was so well trained that all it took was a downward glance from Bob for him to go to the sit position. In one fluid motion, Bob dropped the leash and moved a couple steps in front of Bub. While most of us young rookies in the class figured that was a signal to Bub that he was free to roam the room, not a muscle in his finely tuned body moved. He sat perfectly still and fixed his gaze on his admiring handler. Bob returned the stare and I would have sworn that the two of them were engaged in some strange contest to see who could read the other's mind. This went on for what seemed to all of us an eternity. Bub's eyes glued to Bob, Bob's to Bub. After about two minutes of mutual admiration, Bob ever so effortlessly returned to Bub's left side and gave him a very gentle pat on the head.

A slight variation of the "sit, stay" was the "down, stay." The "down" command required you to gracefully plop to the ground and make yourself comfortable; the dog that is, not the handler. All dogs do this slightly differently, but for me, think of a frog without the scales and you have a mental picture of me in the down position. Mom and Dad loved one particular picture of me comfortably resting in a carpet of lush green grass in front of our house in my frog position.

Back to the class. Once again, Bob turned to his partner in crime to demonstrate the "down, stay" command. With the slightest movement of his right arm out in front of the dog, Bob motioned and Bub immediately assumed the down position and waited for any further instructions. With a firm "stay" to Bub, Bob began walking slowly away, ending up a good twenty-five yards away at the other end of the ring. You would have thought someone had just explained to Bub that if he did nothing more than blink an eye for the next two minutes that he would be sent a lifetime supply of rawhides. I never saw a dog lie so peacefully, yet so attentively. After two minutes of pure silence, Bob shouted "come" and within nanoseconds Bub mysteriously appeared in a sit position in front of Bob's size-thirteen feet.

Now it was our turn to try this out. What ensued looked like a scene from *Animal House*, only this one involving real live animals out of control. Let's just say none of us came close to pulling off the perfection demonstrated by the Bob and Bub show. Some of the pups simply followed their unsuspecting handlers down to the other end of the ring as soon as the owners began walking away. Others lasted in the down position for the amount of time it took the handlers to make their way to the other end and then they proceeded to saunter over and have a chat with the dog next to them. Without a doubt, all of us were works in progress.

Over the next few weeks, and with the requisite time devoted to homework, my classmates and I eventually learned the basic commands. The last night of class was our final exam. Just as an instructor made up a key with all of the answers to the exam, Bob used

Bub for the same purpose. He took the handsome Pinscher through his paces without a single miscue and it was obvious when they were finished what an A+ paper looked like.

While none of us got a letter grade, each of our handlers received a sheet from Bob at the end of the night with some feedback on what we did right, what we needed to improve on, and so forth. It was a proud moment for all of us when Bob passed out our diplomas to our handlers and gave a gentle pat on the head to each of us new grads. The inscription on my certificate read:

Congratulations!
This is to certify that Duffy Porter has been awarded a B.S. from Bob's Canine College.

When we returned home, Dad was eagerly waiting for us at the front door. You would have thought I had graduated magna cum laude from Harvard the way he doted over me. I was beaming from ear to ear at my accomplishment. As Mom admiringly showed off my certificate, Dad asked her what the B.S. stood for. Mom very nonchalantly explained that in my particular case I had been awarded the prestigious "Bachelor of Sorts"! Given my passage into neuterhood, as I so painstakingly described earlier, what could have been more appropriate!

The fact that Dad wasn't able to help see me through the first class ended up being the reason I received a second degree. The folks figured the training was just as important for them as it was for me. So before even a few weeks had passed, off I marched again, this time with Dad in tow to see my buddies Bob and Bub.

The routine was pretty similar, although I felt like an old pro compared to many of the rookies in the class. I sailed through the class with flying colors and, when the last class was over, I received my second diploma. Okay. So I could understand why I had been awarded a *bachelor's* degree. But now this advanced degree? Sure, as I explained earlier on, the folks made certain I took care of my business prior to each night's class. But still, why would this warrant the degree I received? I will never know, but there it was, my MBA, a master's degree in business administering.

Ah, life in the burbs!

Eleven

SUBURBIA

Once I had passed into neuterhood and received a proper education, I settled into a relatively peaceful existence in the suburbs. In fact, the first ten years of my life were spent in the burbs of a big Midwestern city. Life was good.

Maybe you are familiar with the suburban life-style. The nine-to-five routine during the week. Pizza on Friday nights. Dry cleaning to drop off or pick up and other errands to run on Saturdays. Either out for a movie, or, better yet for my money, rent a flick on Saturday nights. Out for a nice romp on Sunday mornings and then some grocery shopping. Back at it again on Monday mornings. Okay, the folks back at it, while I recovered from an action-packed weekend.

As I mentioned earlier, Mom was in sales and

Dad was a professor. Let's just say that they both were in careers that suited their personalities. I swear, Mom could have sold a pair of fins and a wetsuit to a Labrador retriever. Not in the least bit by appearance, but by sheer tenacity, she was the bulldog of the family. Yes, sir, Mom was one of the finest sales persons East of the Mississippi and she worked a territory that reached all the way over to the mighty river.

If Mom was the Bulldog of the family, then Dad was the Border Collie. Training was his life. As a college professor he spent his life trying to mold young minds. Dad taught at a university in the city and took the train to work. One of my favorite times of the day was when Mom loaded me up after she returned home from work and we drove down to the station to meet Dad coming home on the 5:05. When he stepped down off the train I reacted just like all of the other kids down there to meet their pops, licking him in the face as if he was a sailor returning from five years away at sea.

Because Dad was a professor, there were days when he didn't have to make the long trek downtown to teach classes. Instead he could spend those days at home, doing his research and grading exams. Naturally, this arrangement suited me just fine. With my two degrees in hand, I felt more than qualified to be his able graduate assistant. We hung out together in his office, him shuffling through papers and me curled up at his feet. Though he never asked my opinion, I always felt ready if he had any questions on what grades to assign to the big stack of papers that were a constant fixture on his desk.

Eventually the time came when Mom no longer went to an office every day. In business jargon, she became "mobile." At first I wasn't sure what to make of this. From our daily runs I had no doubt about her mobility. But this was apparently something quite different. The bottom line was that Mom started spending more time at home with me. Professor Pops home some days during the week and mobile Mom home every day. This arrangement suited me just fine.

Not that the three of us were couch potatoes out in the burbs. Quite the contrary. Mom and Dad were dedicated runners and they made certain that Sonny joined them on their daily romps. I wouldn't have wanted it any other way. In my youth it was mostly me pulling them along. I set the pace. But as you well know there comes that time in the accelerated life of a dog when all of a sudden he is now older than his parents. Strange concept, isn't it? As I got up there in years I slowed down like any senior citizen would, but I never hesitated to bolt for the door when I saw the two of them lace up their running shoes.

Our runs weren't limited to our daily jaunts in the neighborhood. On weekends we often drove around the area to compete in road races. If you have never been to a road race, you wouldn't believe what goes on at these spectacles. Hundreds, or sometimes even thousands, of scantily-clad middle-aged yuppies run around suburban neighborhoods, with no apparent purpose in mind than claiming a T-shirt given out to every finisher. The folks' T-shirt collection was already sizeable when I came along and it grew to unmanageable proportions during my time with them. Over the years they became walking advertisements for every conceivable business within a hundred-mile radius, thanks to the names plastered on the backs of those shirts.

The distances that we needed to run to secure one of the coveted T-shirts varied considerably. Dad ran the occasional marathon, but Mom and I showed more common sense and stuck with the shorter distances. Why torture yourself through 26.2 miles for a T-shirt when you could get one for running a 5K?

I must admit that I never quite understood the fascination with the whole kilometer thing. What genius decided that a race ought to cover 3.1 miles instead of just three miles? What was that last one-tenth of a mile supposed to prove, anyway? Ah, the strange habits of two-leggeds!

Whenever I ran the 5Ks with Mom she made sure that I had plenty of opportunity to do my business before the starting gun went off. To tell the truth, I preferred the more civilized races that used a horn or some similar device to signal the start. Guns always made me a bit nervous, especially in the hands of some guy standing in front of a few thousand people.

Anyhow, back to my pre-race routine. Taking care of my business before the start of a race proved to be a distinct advantage. Being the private sort, I wasn't keen on the idea of relieving myself along the race course, not to mention the lost seconds on our quest to place in our age group. While they often provided them for humans, I never once saw a port-a-pup strategically placed along a race course.

Once the races were underway I was focused entirely on the goal. Mom always had to work hard to rein me in during the first few hundred yards or so, my tendency being to see just how fast I could get out of the gate. Some of the bigger races sent out a "rabbit." When I first heard about the rabbit my appetite was naturally whetted, and this only fed my instincts to take off like a bat out of hell. It took me awhile to understand that the rabbit wasn't anything resembling what the name implied. This was just another one of those stupid names that humans give to something that looks nothing like what it is named after. The rabbit in a road race turned out to be some human merely sent out to set the pace. No wonder I never picked up the scent of the rabbit in these races.

Naturally, a highlight for me was the post-race parties. I especially liked the races that catered to those of us running along on four legs. That didn't necessarily mean the canines walked away with a T-shirt, but we normally scored a very impressive goodie bag, full of delectable treats. Forget the T-shirts. I never thought they were designed for a dog's physique in the first place. When the festivities were over, I hopped into the back of our Sit Up Vertically, carrying my goodie bag, knowing that I had run a good race.

So you can see that life in suburbia was good to me. I was physically fit, getting two squares a day, not to mention the regular treats, and as an only dog all the attention imaginable from my two adoring parents.

Twelve

HAVE YOUR DOGS CALL
MY DOGS (HEAVEN)

"What you reading there, Rex?" I inquired of my black-and-white Terrier buddy one fine morning. Even though I had been up here well short of an eternity, we had established such a good rapport I didn't think twice about interrupting him. Still, the look on his face led me to believe he was preoccupied with something.

"Wonder of wonders, but I finally got a reply to the query letter," Rex said, his bullet head still buried in its contents.

Six months had passed and he was yet to receive a single response to his query, even though he emailed it along with my first four chapters to every editor who had ever shown the slightest interest in the canine world. While Rex grew more and more impatient with every passing day, I had continued to make progress on my tale and was less bothered by what Rex considered a personal affront.

"What does it say, Rex? Do they want to publish my tale?" I perked up, suddenly aware of the significance of this email to the future of my story.

"Here. You can read it for yourself," Rex said, showing the letter to me. "Somebody in New York finally had the courtesy to at least reply."

With Rex's noncommittal response, I immediately started reading the letter, deciding I would have to form my own opinion whether the editor was impressed or not.

My Dear Rex:

Allow me to introduce myself and my company. Penelope Pendergrast Press produces, prints, publishes, and promotes a plethora of pleasing poetry and prose for the pure pleasure of the perpetually persnickety perusing public. All alliteration aside, I begin with my sincerest apology for taking so long to respond. As you well know, dogs are hot right now and we have more queries than we can possibly handle. Regardless, I try to personally respond to each one I receive.

Let me start by saying that your client obviously knows how to turn a phrase, providing the reader with a rather witty take on life as a dog. And he has a compelling story to tell, a true rags to riches account, from the young protagonist's start in a hayloft to his eventual adoption.

Certainly every good story has to have a distinctive voice. And as I understand, your client knows his stuff, having worked at a shelter. But let me cut directly to the chase, my dear Rex. According to our good friend Webster, a voice is a sound coming from the mouth, and I for one have always took that to mean the frontal cavity on one of our own species, not one on a dog.

Frankly the "first dog" thing is unsettling to me. Unfortunately I have the same uneasy feeling with the canine point of view. We live today in a world of skeptics, people only believing what they can see. Witness the plethora of reality TV shows. I can appreciate that your client has employed the first-person dog point of view to bring the reader closer to the action. Still, I have grave doubts that anyone will take seriously a story written by a talking dog. Readers want to believe, not make believe; at least that is my considered opinion. Sorry, but I guess I am just not into anthropomorphizing a dog.

I hope you take no offense to my candor. I see exceptional promise in your budding author and would be happy to see a revised version of the manuscript in the third person written from his point of view rather than that of the dog.

Do let me know what you think of my suggestion. In fact, daaaahling, why don't you have your dogs call my dogs and we can do lunch sometime?

Sincerely,

Penelope Pendergrast

"Now what do we do?" I asked, giving the letter back to Rex.

"Well, in case you hadn't noticed, Duff, the old gal hasn't the slightest clue that I am a dog, or for that matter that my client is one as well. For all she knows, I live down the street from her and can 'do lunch' at the drop of a hat. For all she knows, you are a human sitting right now in front of your laptop, pouring your guts out on a new book. And she is happy to meet with me. All we need to do is agree to change from the first dog to the third dog and adopt a human point of view. I can easily make up some excuse about not being able to meet for lunch. That is not the question. The question is whether you want to write your tale from the viewpoint of a human, rather than from your own perspective. That is your call, old chap. What do you think? I have no dogs that can call her dogs, but I can certainly email her with a response."

I waited for some time before responding to Rex's question. I had poured my heart and soul into telling my tale and now some editor in New York wanted me to make believe that someone else was telling my story. It was all so confusing. I was beginning to wonder why I ever wanted to do this in the first place.

"Rex, for starters, should I be offended at being

called a protagonist, especially one in a hayloft?"

"Not at all, my man, that just means you are the main character in your story. Nothing to take offense at there," Rex chuckled.

"Fine. But being accused of anthropomorphizing a dog?"

"Don't worry about that either, Duff, it just means she doesn't believe in attributing human characteristics to a dog."

"Terrific," I responded with a hint of disdain in my very dogly voice, "but why do some people feel the need to throw around big words?"

"I wish I could answer that one, Duff, but having spent my whole life as a dog rather than a person, I'm afraid I don't have a good answer."

"Big words aside, Rex, I understand what she is asking me to do. She wants me to make believe that a human is telling my tale. It just doesn't sound right to me. This is my story and who better to tell it than me? Why should we make believe that someone else is telling it when both of us know it is me? No, I just can't do it. This is my story and I am the only one qualified to tell it."

"So be it," Rex replied in a tone of resignation as he turned and walked away.

Regardless of whether Rex shared my strong

feeling about person and point of view, he knew me well enough by now to know that this point wasn't negotiable. Rex had my blessing to do lunch with the gal, but *I* had a story to tell and it wouldn't be some third person, but rather *I*, the lively Bull Terrier mix, that would be the one to tell it.

Who says you need graham crackers to make s'mores? Try substituting a dog biscuit if you really want a treat.

Thirteen
SUMMER CAMP

Yes, life in the suburbs suited me just fine. Early on I found out how lucky I was to have folks who took me with them nearly everywhere they went. Whether it was to the grocery store or for a weekend getaway, I went along. Throw me in the back of the Sit Up Vertically and I couldn't be happier. It mattered little to me where we were going—assuming it wasn't to the vet for some alterations—as long as I was allowed to go.

We all learn in life that there are exceptions to every rule. The exception for me was when the folks traveled in one of those big birds in the sky. I never flew. Even after a hard 5K I still tipped the scales at about forty pounds, well over the limit for a dog to ride in a crate under a passenger's seat. And there was no way that the folks would have allowed me to ride in steerage in the belly of a 747, like some cast-away. So even though I traveled to just about every part of the lower forty-eight, I never flew.

On those occasions when they did fly, Mom had a standard answer when someone invariably asked, "So what did you do with Duff?"

"Oh, he's at summer camp," she would proudly proclaim as if I was a Boy Scout sent off to earn merit badges.

I will never forget the first time I went off to "camp." I had been living at home for the better part of a year and the folks were taking a trip that required them to fly. I am not sure who it was more traumatic for: me or them. Since landing in my new digs I had barely been out of their sight for more than a few hours at a time, and here they were getting ready to leave me for a week with some stranger.

The ride out to camp was pleasant enough. We passed farms and fields with Holsteins munching away on fresh alfalfa in the pastures. It seemed like we were just out for another of our Sunday drives through the bucolic countryside.

Think again. As soon as we turned into the driveway I knew something wasn't quite kosher. A chorus of howls greeted us, a pack of Hounds speeding alongside as we approached the parking lot. As the dust from the gravel road settled, Dad shut off the engine and all became eerily quiet. The folks seemed particularly somber as they made their way out of the car. As soon as I leaped out the back, there were new smells everywhere. Being a male I made certain to mark at least a couple of spots. You know, basically what humans do when they leave a calling card.

We were met at the door by a pleasant woman. She introduced herself, shook hands with the folks, and gave me a pat on the head. She tried to reassure the folks that everything would be just fine, although you could see from the looks on the faces of Mom and Dad that they weren't so sure. Eventually the lady broke the ice and said something I recall to this day: "Well, you stay here with Duff and I will go on your vacation."

At that point, they all had a good chuckle and the folks seemed to relax a bit. Fighting back tears, they each gave me a little smooch on the nose and off they went.

The nice lady gave me a gentle coaxing on the end of my lead but I "put on the brakes." I found out later that this was the cutesy expression to describe what happens when a dog would rather not go where he or she is being asked to go. Although the "camp coun-selor" was gentle with her corrections, I could tell that she meant business. From my extensive training with the Bob and Bub show I knew the meaning of a correction just as much as the next dog. I soon released my parking brake and followed her down the long narrow hallway.

The perky woman led me into an open kennel and closed the door behind me. My first thought was that this place bore an eerie resemblance to the shelter where I landed for adoption. It was mass chaos. Dozens of dogs howling at the top of their lungs every time someone like me came in for the first time. A somewhat institutional smell to the joint, it lacked the comforts I had grown accustomed to at my new home. Suffice it to say that it took me awhile to fall asleep that first night.

Embarrassing as it might sound, Mom called the kennel to check in on me at least a couple times during my stays. Not wanting to be teased by the other dogs, I tried to ignore it when the nice lady came by and let me know that Mom had called to see how I was getting along. After all, your bunkmates on either side could be pretty cruel when it came to this sort of thing. Still, deep down, it was nice to hear about those calls and know that the folks hadn't forgotten about me, and that they fully intended to return for me.

I shouldn't give you the wrong impression about "camp." There were no canoe trips down the river, no cookouts over the campfire with all of us howling folk songs. No, in many respects camp wasn't all that different from life at the shelter. You got to know the dog on either side of you and could compare notes. What's your favorite rawhide? Do you have a favorite toy? What are your accommodations like back home, that sort of thing. Of course, the major difference between shelter and camp was knowing that the folks would be coming back for you, at least after the first time I was sent off to camp.

After what seemed like an eternity, the day finally came when I would be going home. The day started in an unusual fashion with a bath. After a few more stays at the kennel, I eventually cracked the code: Bath = Going Home. What could be sweeter!

Much like that day when the folks first came to see me at the shelter, I bounded for joy when they picked me up, bouncing from Mom to Dad, back to Mom, and on and on until they gently hinted to me that it was time to go home. But once home, I pouted for a good day or two. This was my not-so-subtle way to let the two of them know that I didn't really appreciate being left behind. The nice lady also said that I might sleep a bit more than usual when I got home. As she put it, "They always sleep with one eye open here." I am not sure what the heck she meant by this, but she was right on. I slept like a young pup the first couple of days after going home, all the while dreaming of my time at summer camp but also glad to be back home.

You will find a bowl of fresh Perrier and a
supply of rawhides in your room.
Do let us know, sir, if there is anything we
can do to make your stay more enjoyable.

Fourteen

SMALL PETS

So it came to pass. A peaceful life in the suburbs with an occasional visit to camp. But as I said earlier, the three of us traveled together quite often as well. Many of our jaunts were of the weekend variety, although we did take some longer excursions.

Depending on our destination, we sometimes stayed with relatives or friends. But more often than not, we stayed somewhere along the road. Don't take me too literally here. It is not as if we just pulled over and slept alongside the highway. Besides, the folks were never the type to camp. No pup tent for them, although an abode by this name had a certain sort of appeal to me.

Speaking of names, I was always tickled by the names that humans give to the various places they sleep. Hotels, motels, inns, B & Bs, and on and on.

All of them simply being places that put a roof over your head and allow you to get some shuteye before embarking on your next adventure. Over the years we stayed at every type of abode you can imagine.

Rarely did we just wait to look for a room until we were ready to pull over for the night. Being organized, the folks planned ahead. Okay, *Mom* planned ahead, and it was she who made all of the arrangements, all the reservations. I swear the woman had AAA tour books for every state in the union. Those books were a good starting point in her quest to find suitable housing for the three of us along the highways and byways of this great nation. And it was always left to Mom to make a case as to why *I* should be allowed to stay in the room with them. Suffice it to say that this was something that she found very challenging at times, a challenge she always seemed up to.

Over time, Mom developed a certain technique when she called to make reservations. Dad and I waited patiently on the sidelines. We became adept at learning how things were going without ever hearing the voice on the other end of the phone line. Imagine the old Bob Newhart skit, where you heard what he said but not what the person on the other end did. The conversation might go something like this:

"Hi, I was calling to see what you had available for

the nights of June third through the fifth."

"You do, that's great, because I know this is starting to get into your busy season. We would need a queen, preferably a king. And if you have one, a room with a Jacuzzi and a fireplace."

"Terrific, and with the AAA discount, what is your rate?"

"Fair enough, do you offer a continental breakfast?"

"Sounds good, and oh, by the way, do you take *small* pets?"

Always, the emphasis was on the word "small." This was Mom's way of reassuring the innkeepers that I wasn't some dog with the dimensions of a Shetland pony. This of course was the question Mom had wanted an answer to from the very beginning of the conversation. But for psychological reasons she always left it to the end. Her way of thinking was that it was best not to start off the conversation by asking if they "took dogs." Better to warm up the innkeeper and get all of the other details ironed out before getting to the deal breaker. Anyway, if the answer to the "small pet" question was yes, then that pretty much was the end of the phone call. Maybe give them a credit card to guarantee the first night and tell them how much we were looking forward to staying at their fine establishment.

When there was hesitation or a flat out "no" coming from the other end of the line, these conversations got interesting. Dad and I listened attentively in the background, almost knowing how it would go from there on out.

"No, gee, I thought you probably did. Most of the _____ (fill in the blank with your favorite hotel chain) that we have stayed in take a dog. Well, I can assure you that my dog is better behaved than any kids that stay at your hotel. He doesn't cry in the middle of the night and I guarantee you that he won't spit up or pee on the carpet."

It was beyond Mom's comprehension why a place would take a kid but not a dog. Being the persistent type, at this point, she asked to speak to the manager. Also being the persuasive type, she would often convince the manager that I would not be a problem. She reassured him or her that I was well groomed, got my feet wiped every time I came in from outside—something that was the absolute truth—and that I slept in my own crate. This was also the truth. Everywhere we traveled, my crate went along. It was my home on wheels, a dog's version of a Winnebago. I liked having my crate along on road trips. Regardless of how strange or foreign a hotel room might be, sleeping in my crate made it feel more like home.

At other times, the dialogue took a different turn.

"You take small pets, but only in the smoking rooms? Why would I want a smoking room? My dog doesn't smoke!"

With this one, Dad and I would be rolling around on the floor in stitches. My dog doesn't smoke. Good one, Mom! This was another policy that she couldn't comprehend. What was the possible rationale for allowing dogs, but only in the smoking rooms? Did they think dogs really do smoke? It reminded me of that famous set of paintings where all of the dogs are sitting around playing poker, some of them smoking big stogies. Anyway, when they said they allowed dogs, but only in smoking rooms, this was usually the end of the conversation. There was no way the three of us would be staying in a room that had been smoked in.

Another thing Mom sometimes faced was the fact that they wanted to charge some ridiculous amount for me. She would remind them that I did in fact sleep in my crate and that I would not need my own bed. Didn't matter, they said, the additional amount was required to "clean up" after a dog had been in a room. This also flabbergasted her. What did they think I was going to do in the room, anyway? She reminded them that I went outside to do my business.

No matter, that would be another twenty-five dollars a night for Fido. Or in some cases there would be a deposit. This was fair enough and usually not a problem for Mom, since she knew I wasn't going to trash the room, like you might expect from a group of college kids in Fort Lauderdale or Cancun on spring break.

Over the years it was surprising to learn the places that would and would not take a dog. The ones that did usually advertised themselves as being "Pet Friendly." You know, the ones with a little doggie icon in their advertisements, right next to the symbol letting you know they have high-speed Internet in all the rooms. To be reduced to an icon was a bit of an insult but, hey, what can you do?

What was beyond belief was some of the places that were not "Pet Friendly." We're talking some real dumps. The no-tell motel types of places. The type that had shag carpeting left over from the seventies. The type with a bedspread so dingy that my folks didn't even want *me* lying on it. What a dog could possibly do to some of these rat-infested places was beyond comprehension, but such was the case.

On the other end of the spectrum, I stayed in some of the nicest hotels in the land in my time, some real five-star palaces. Once, Mom had a recognition event at a swank hotel in the downtown of a big city. Not only was I allowed to stay, but everyone there treated me like royalty. The doorman, true to his name, opened the door for me. I didn't press my luck, but I'm guessing if I had walked up to the concierge I would have been shown a list of all the plays in town featuring dogs in them.

Once we got up to the room, I discovered treats waiting for me along with a dog bowl filled with Perrier. There was turn-down service in the evenings. That meant a chocolate for the folks and an extra biscuit for me. I was the epitome of the pampered pooch and I loved every minute of it. The only bummer came when it was time to check out and go back to the ordinary life of a suburban dog.

Some of my favorite memories are from those days spent on the road with my folks. Boy, did we ever have fun. Looking back now, I know those times wouldn't have been near the fun if Mom had not been so persistent. If she hadn't been able to convince all of those innkeepers that I was in fact a small pet, that I did in fact sleep in my own bed, and that, no, I did not smoke.

**Ladies and gentlemen,
now entering the ring, the mutts!**

Fifteen
BEST IN SHOW

Now I don't want to give you the impression that I spent all of my time either at camp or out on the road. To the contrary, many a night found me curled up on one of my favorite pillows that the folks placed strategically around the house. I especially loved to do my curling up during those harsh Midwestern winters.

Every February brought one of the real traditions to our house in the burbs. Mom and Dad would check the listings, clear their calendars, and settle in for two evenings of must-see television. I am talking of course about the granddaddy of all dog shows, the Westminster from Madison Square Garden in the Big Apple.

I can tell you that in my first year in my new home this spectacle held about as much appeal for me as a root canal. Right up there with getting your glands cleared. And if you are either a dog or a dog owner, you know the glands I am talking about. All of this adulation showered on a few pampered pooches. *Give me a break.*

I remember the first time it came on. I had arrived in September at my new digs and after a few months I was beginning to feel pretty comfortable. After all, I was getting two meals a day, not counting the occasional pig's hoof, plenty of exercise to keep the body and mind in sync, and best of all I had a roof over my head. All in all, not a bad setup for a stray that had spent six months in a shelter with relatively few prospects for the future.

It was one of those typically bitter winter evenings. Even so, I was a bit surprised when Dad started hauling in firewood from the back porch. Usually a fire was reserved for the weekends, either when the folks rented a movie on a Saturday night or when Dad plopped down for a Sunday afternoon of NFL football. But here it was a Monday night, a school night, if you will. Before long Dad had a roaring fire going. I had just polished off a rawhide and settled into my typical spot close enough to feel the warmth emanating from our fireplace but not so close as to singe the coarse white hair on my back.

As Dad grabbed for the remote, I waited patiently to see what we might be watching. Maybe the latest sitcom or a college basketball game. Well, you can only imagine my surprise when I heard the announcement that the Westminster Kennel Club's Dog Show was now beaming live from Madison Square Garden in New York City!

Now I am thinking to myself, what in the world is a dog show? I'd heard of car shows, boat shows, RV shows, and other public displays of affection for toys that humans treat themselves to, but a dog show? This sounded like the most demeaning thing imaginable. Are they somehow going to lift the hood on a dog and take a look inside? I mean, Madison Square Garden, home of the Knickerbockers, and they are going to parade a bunch of dogs through this venerable arena? Better have plenty of pooper scoopers on hand.

Before long I started to understand what was going on here. The announcer explained that over the next two nights a competition would take place to see which dog, among the hundreds assembled, would be worthy of the title Best in Show. A Miss America contest for canines, if you will. But what about the males among us? Was there any place for the guys in this production? And this assumed that none of the pooches were married, right? What kind of contest were they running here, anyway?

I could tell early on that this was a totally different kind of spectacle than anything I had ever witnessed before. No question about that. The guy on the TV explained that preliminary judging had already pared down the contestants to the winner in each of the hundred-plus breeds. For example, the top Beagle had been chosen, the best Bulldog, the champion Dalmation; you get the picture. Each of the hundred-plus breeds was then categorized into one of a number of groups, such as the Terriers and the Hounds.

Now it was time to parade out each of the winners and pick the top dog in each of the groups. The announcer methodically explained that you can't compare a Beagle and a Bassett, for example, but rather that you are trying to figure out which one of the winners best exemplifies the best from that breed. That is, you are judging that winner against the standard for that particular breed. If the Beagle best represented the breed standard, then he or she would go to carry the banner for the Hound group to crown the Best in Show.

But where in the world did they get some of these group names? The Hound and Terrier groups were pretty easy to understand. And, okay, the sporting group. But the non-sporting group? How demoralizing must it be to be told that you are non-sporting? Does this mean that you aren't a good sport? Or that you are a total dork and inept when it comes to playing any sports? Really. And what about the toy group, those little designer dogs? The kind celebrities carry around in their purses. You want to talk about demeaning. How would you like it if your lot in life had been reduced to being some human's toy?

I tell you, this was a different sort of TV program from any I had witnessed. Even the commercials were different. Instead of trying to sell beer or cars like they do during the breaks in a football game, Madison Avenue was going after dog owners, pushing dog food, dog toys, you name it, any product connected to the canine world. I swear that at one point during one of the more heart-throbbing ads, I looked over and Mom was reaching for the tissue.

The folks seemed highly entertained by this public display of affection for us canines. Although I still thought this a fairly strange form of entertainment, I decided to go along with them and have fun with it, too. What choice did I have, anyway? I had never been put in charge of the remote and didn't figure this was the time for me to ask either.

The first night proceeded with the selection of winners in four of the groups. The announcer urged everyone to be sure to tune in the next night when the remaining group winners would be picked as well as the coveted Best in Show. Naturally, I was disappointed that the mixed breed group winner wasn't chosen the first night, but by this time in my life I had already come to recognize patience as a virtue. "My people" would have to wait until the following night.

By the end of the show we were all ready for bed. When I trotted into my crate I noticed an extra pat or two on the old noggin. I took this as a reaction to the folks having just spent three hours looking at some fine examples of my species. Anyway, I was tuckered out from all of the festivities and knew that I would be off in la-la land the instant my head hit the pillow....

"Ladies and gentlemen, would you please welcome the mixed breed group now entering the ring."

Even though Mom just took me outside for one last tinkle—not the easiest thing to pull off in Midtown Manhattan—I have a feeling that I could stand to relieve myself one more time. Forget it. We are next in line to enter the show ring and there is no turning back. My stomach is churning and I'm as nervous as a Dachshund in a room full of Dobermans.

The bright lights make it feel like the dead of summer even though it is February. The crowd has worked itself into a frenzy as if they have been waiting all along for the mixed breed group. We parade into the arena like a herd of stampeding buffalo and make one pass around the ring. We each settle into our assigned spots, easily identifiable by our benches with the name of our breed on them. Thankfully for me, the breeds are arranged in alphabetical order and I won't have to wait long to make my pass by the judge. I hear the public address announcer's voice again over the loudspeaker:

"A mix of the Bull Terrier, the Jack Russell Terrier, and the Rat Terrier, the Bull-Jack-Rat, or the BJR, as it is affectionately known, originated in, well to be honest, we are not sure where. England? France? The colonies? We really don't have a clue. They come in a variety of shapes and sizes, but their coarse, white hair is a trademark of the breed. Clownish in disposition, the BJR is also a loyal guardian and in the hands of the right owner makes a wonderful companion. This is BJR Number 57."

Overall, not a bad introduction, but I have no time to dwell on such formalities. Some guy in a tuxedo is making his way towards Mom and me. I thought such getups were generally reserved for weddings and bar mitzvahs, but nonetheless the next thing I know, the guy in the penguin suit has his hand inside my mouth. My first reaction is to give him the best signal I know to kindly remove his hand, but I come to my senses and realize that he is just giving me the once over.

Next he is running his hands along my belly. I must say, a bit embarrassing to have some guy checking out your private parts in front of an assembled crowd numbering in the thousands, but again, what can I do under the circumstances? Go easy there, big guy. I just had some new stitch work done a few months ago. Fortunately he doesn't dwell long on my chassis and now he is instructing Mom to trot me around the ring once, counterclockwise. I hope Mom has her senses about her, because with my jitters I can't think straight enough to remember which way those blasted hands on a clock move.

We make our grand march once around the ring and the crowd goes nuts. I am in fine form now and realize that it is in my best interest to give the fans a show. Every muscular inch of my finely tuned body is busting with pride as I effortlessly trot in rhythm to the cadence of claps coming from the audience. Once back to our bench I realize that the cameras are now off Mom and me. The announcer has turned the crowd's attention to the cute little Cockapoo standing next to me.

It seems an eternity before the judge has made his way around to prod, poke, and in every way imaginable examine all of us mixed breeds. But eventually the prelims are over and he begins to selectively pull some of the dogs out for further examination. A handsome Bullmation gets a nod from the penguin. The Labradoodle springs forward when he hears his name called. A Ratshire Terrier takes her place in the finalists' circle. It is a relief to know that at least a relative of mine has made the cut. Then, wouldn't you know it, the gal next to me, the little Cockapoo, is pulled out. I figure this is the end of the road, but to my amazement the judge motions to Mom to bring me forward. At this point, my heart is racing. But I keep telling myself to remain calm. Be cool.

One by one, the judge gives each of us another steely-eyed look. Didn't the penguin's mother ever tell him that it isn't polite to stare? Eventually he instructs each of us, in order, to make one more pass around the show ring. Since I was the last dog pulled out, Mom and I are the last to make our encore march. When our turn finally comes, the crowd goes nuts. I am now in my finest form, well aware of which way is counterclockwise, and I take the lead, pulling Mom along after me. I glance out of the corner of one eye and see that everyone is now out of their seats and roaring in thunderous applause as I parade around the ring one last time. Even so, I can hear my heart pounding when we finally end up back at our bench, the one proudly proclaiming my breed, the BJR.

The judge makes one more pass by each of us handsome speci-mens and then stops in his tracks in front of me. He seems suspended in time for an instant and then he nods to Mom to pull me up front. The cute Cockapoo follows in behind us, and then my cousin, the Ratshire Terrier. The judge tells all of us assembled that this is how the ribbons will be handed out. One more time the crowd goes bananas. At this point, all of the mixed breeds and their handlers surround Mom and me, congratulating us on a well-deserved victory.

The TV cameras cut away for a commercial and a woman with a microphone in her hand is walking towards us. She gives me a *pat on the head and explains to Mom that as soon as they are back from a commercial she would like to interview us. Now my heart resumes its pounding. Before I have much time to even primp just a bit, the woman is back with her mike shoved up in Mom's face and a camera beats down on the two of us.*

"Congratulations on a hard-fought win out there. This little BJR really seemed to be in fine form tonight!"

"Thank you. Yes, we have been pointing to this show ever since we adopted this guy from the shelter back in the fall," Mom explained, barely able to catch her breath. "Duff seemed to play off the crowd and respond to their applause for him. I am proud of him and the way he carried himself tonight."

"Tell us, how does it feel to be representing the mixed breed group, to know you are going up against all of those purebreds for the coveted title? As you know, in the storied history of this show, no mixed breed has ever taken home the Best in Show."

"I couldn't be prouder—of this little guy, of the BJR breed, and all of the mixed breeds out there. We will do our best to represent all of the mixes of the world. I suppose there is a first time for every-thing," Mom offered.

"Hi, Duff, wake up. Boy, you must have really been sleeping hard."

I recognized this voice immediately as the same one that had just been answering the reporter's questions. But now Mom isn't dressed in her finest duds, but rather in her PJs. And I'm not standing in the middle of Madison Square Garden, but just stretching as I make my way out of my crate. So much for all the hoopla. All of the excitement must have set me off on a real whopper of a dream. It was as if I had scarfed down a box of chocolates before hitting the hay. Oh well, hope is what dreams are for, that maybe someday they will let mixed breeds into the Westminster and that I will be called upon to represent all of us mongrels for Best in Show. What is that expression humans have? When pigs can fly?

**Spare me the indignity. None of that
invisible fencing nonsense for Yours Truly.**

Sixteen

A HOUSE IN
THE COUNTRY

After a few years living in town, the folks decided
I needed more room to roam. So we built a house
in the country. Don't take me too literally. We *had* a
house built in the country. Dad stood about as much
chance of building a house as I did of learning to
speak Chinese. To minimize any further blows to his
ego, let's just say he was mechanically challenged and
leave it at that. Regardless of who was pounding the
nails, it was a kick to go out to the site on a regular
basis and see how construction was going. Ah, the
smell of fresh sawdust!

In keeping with the American way, the new house
in the country was bigger than our starter house in
the burbs. Wider doorways and longer hallways meant

that I had even more room to romp. When it came time to furnish Dad's office I was pleased with the hunt motif the folks chose, complete with a picture of a Terrier with his nose buried in a fox hole. There was even a replica of a bugle that hung on the wall. It was obvious that in our few years together I had made quite an impression on Mom and Dad.

I was relieved to see my crate set up in one corner of the kitchen, the same arrangement I had grown accustomed to in town. I was also impressed to find that the folks had actually taken my needs into account in the design of our new digs and left space in the laundry room for me to take my meals.

Most amazing of all, though, was the engineering feat that had been designed just to address my personal needs. Outside the door of the laundry room I had my very own dog run. Not some chain-link fence thrown up around the entire perimeter of the yard, but an area that had been specifically engineered with me in mind.

It was all very tasteful. Off the back steps of the laundry room the dog run was rocked in, my dog house sitting prominently at the far end. A handsome cedar fence surrounded the run with just enough space left between the boards to let the sun through.

The dog run was a godsend in the winter. On

those arctic nights, the folks just opened the door for me rather than going to the trouble of putting on parkas and parading me down the road. The system worked perfectly. I will never forget my first night when they let me out to try the new accommodations. Gazing up at the galaxy of stars as I took one last tinkle, I wondered how life could get any better. While I was hopeful the folks had no intentions of leaving me there for any extended period of time, I grew quite fond of my dog run.

I must report that on occasion I found myself left alone out in the dog run. This happened when the folks hosted a party. For some reason, they thought it best that I view the festivities from a bit of distance. The thought of a lively Bull Terrier running amok with food and drink easily at his disposal was an obvious concern to them. I can't say that I agreed with their thinking, but things could have been worse. Invariably, as these parties wore on, one of the guests would happen to look out the window and spot me. As soon as I made eye contact, I put on my most pitiful look and the guest was putty in my paws. The look that says, "I have been left alone and I am just as miserable out here as the look on my face would seem to indicate."

My technique almost always worked. Before long

the guest would plead to the folks to let in the poor pitiful-looking dog to say hello, and in I would trot. Mission accomplished. Show me to the cheese and crackers.

There were a number of forest preserves close by our house in the country and, you can imagine, these were a favorite destination for me. Plenty of room to roam and take in all of the wonderful fragrances my keen nose immediately picked up. These places were packed with rabbits and squirrels just waiting for a good chase.

In addition to our casual visits to the forest preserve, I always looked forward to the Walk for the Animals. This was a fundraiser for my shelter and naturally the folks were ardent supporters. Every year Mom put her superior sales skills to good use and inevitably wound up as one of the top money-raisers for the walkathon. A professional among amateurs. She took her role in the event very seriously. For weeks leading up to the walk, she carried her pledge sheet in her purse wherever we went. All she had to do was pull out a snapshot of me at my most handsome, and the unsuspecting relative, neighbor, or co-worker was easy prey. Cash or check will work just fine. No plastic, please.

The day of the actual Walk for the Animals was a

hoot. Just being out there at the forest preserve with all of the terrific aromas got my adrenaline pumping. But then to see all of my compatriots marching for a good cause made it even more special. Like me, many of them were alums of the shelter. We were all walking, barking advertisements, not-so-subtle messages that you could indeed find the perfect pooch at a shelter. I always showed up decked out in a favorite bandana, and struck a pose for the cameras whenever the opportunity presented itself.

The only aspect of this love fest that I could never warm up to was the idea of drinking from those communal bowls that the organizers strategically placed along the route. Not to seem snooty, but we all know canines are natural droolers. The thought of lapping up water after who knows how many other dogs had deposited their saliva in it didn't appeal to me. Not terribly civilized, if you ask me. No, I always waited until we got back to the Sit Up Vertically to drink from my own personal water bowl.

As much fun as the walk itself was, I always looked forward with great anticipation to the end of these charity events. At home the folks were very careful about my diet. I swear you would have thought they were training me for the Olympics. No table scraps and all treats were carefully spaced throughout the day. But when we reached the finish line after the walkathon, it was Fido bar the door. All I had to do was saunter over to any one of the many volunteers, flash that winning smile of mine, and, within seconds, I was feasting on every imaginable type of treat ever created for a dog. I suppose I should have felt a bit guilty but, hey, it was all for a good cause.

The Walk for the Animals concluded with a few pictures and an awards ceremony for the top fund-raisers. We always stayed for this, knowing Mom would be toward the top of the leader board. And as I mentioned earlier on, one year Mom won a sitting with a pet photographer. Just as all proud parents do with Jimmy's first school picture, the folks ordered every conceivable size from our session. They got the three-by-fives. They got the five-by-sevens. They got the wallet sizes. They got shots of the three of us. They got candid solo poses of Yours Truly. The centerpiece was an eight-by-eleven that graced the mantle above our fireplace. To this day, I would be willing to bet that, if you asked either one of them, they could still pull out of their wallet one of those pictures to show you.

Yes, the house in the country suited me just fine. With a dog run specifically tailored to meet my most basic needs. The forest preserves were more than I could have ever dreamed of, with an abundance of rabbits and squirrels to keep in line. The fresh air and the starlit nights out in the country were the best. Critters to chase during the day and crickets to serenade me to sleep at night. Life in the country was good.

Warning: Objects in cone are closer
than they appear.

Seventeen

CONEY DOG

I was about ten years old when "it" first appeared. We were still living in the house in the country. We had just come back from one of our brisk morning runs. Of course, that meant it was time for me to turn over on my back and allow Mom to wipe my paws. Humiliating as this might sound, I learned to humor her, knowing that in fact I really had no choice in the matter when it came to my personal hygiene. I was no dummy. I knew who buttered my biscuits.

During this particular normally routine inspection of me, Mom discovered "it." "It" was a small lump growing on my left hind leg. "It" was about the size of a nickel in circumference and was gently protruding from my leg. I'm thinking, *Fair enough, when humans get a blackhead they sterilize a needle, pop the nasty zit, apply a little pancake mix, and move on. So, I will close my eyes, hold my breath, and wait for the signal that the coast is clear.*

I didn't see this as any big deal, but you would have thought aliens had just taken over the country. Immediately Mom sprung into action, on the phone to the vet. The next thing I knew I was being loaded into the back of the Sit Up Vertically.

Ironically, the same guy who assisted—okay, caused— my progression—okay, digression—into neuterhood turned out to be one of our neighbors when we moved to the house in the country. Yes, my vet from my earliest days with Mom and Dad lived just down the road when we settled in the country. I always felt somewhat reassured knowing that, in case of emergency, my personal physician was barely a stone's throw away.

Once at the vet's office I was shuffled into one of the examining rooms with Mom and Dad. They never liked to send me in on my own, and frankly I was always happy for the company. Not that the vet allowed them to have a front row seat for everything. For instance, I was always one of those dogs who never took kindly to having my toenails trimmed. The vet would try to trim them in the main examining room, but if I proved too much of a nuisance, he picked me up like a sack of potatoes and informed the folks to sit tight and that he and I would be back in a jiff. The jiff was just long enough for him to haul me back to another room where I would be unceremoniously fitted with a muzzle. I don't know any kinder and gentler name for the device. For obvious reasons, the vet was much more successful in giving me a puppy manicure when I was wearing a muzzle.

Anyhow, on this particular visit there was no talk about trimming the toenails. Not even a hint of the need to check the old glands, something for which I was grateful. Instead, all attention seemed to be focused on this nickel-sized protrusion on my hind leg. Trying to sound reassuring, the vet told them that "it" was probably nothing to worry about, but best to have "it" removed and sent to the lab for testing.

That was all the folks needed to hear, that qualified reassurance from the vet that "it" was probably nothing to worry about. This was their license to start worrying, and I don't think the worrying ever stopped with them the rest of my life. You see, I was susceptible to these little "its" on my body and, every time one arose, they began worrying. At any rate, the vet informed us—I swear he was looking at me as much as he was them—that we should schedule a time for my surgery.

What is it about "it" that so worries humans? Worries them so much that they go around referring to it as "it" rather than by the "C" word? People go out of their way to refer to "it" by every imaginable word except cancer. Old Duff—really, I wasn't *that* old yet—has a lump. A bump. A bulge. A cyst. A mass. A growth. You name it, there was always some word other than the big "C" word. Let's face it. I had a tumor that needed to be removed.

The morning of the surgery arrived and I gobbled down my breakfast in my usual fashion, as if I had no clue where my next meal would come from. I should have known better. It came from the big tub under the counter, just as it had every other day since I was old enough to remember. Anyway, this morning I was invited to hop into the back of the Sit Up Vertically. You could have heard the proverbial pin drop. Neither Mom nor Dad said a word and they just sat gazing out the window as we drove down the road. As we pulled into the parking lot I very quickly recognized my surroundings.

Once inside we were shuffled off to one of the examining rooms. An assistant took a quick listen to my ticker and did a few other routine tests. As she lifted me down off the table the folks each gave me a big hug and turned to leave. I could see tears in their eyes as they reassured me all would be fine. This all had the feeling like that fateful day years earlier when I was led back into one of the inner rooms and came out a changed man. Well, okay, a changed dog, but you know what I am referring to here.

After some sleep-inducing drugs were pumped into my system, I was out like a light. When I awoke, the vet was looking me over and patting me on the head. That same fancy stitch work that he had performed on my private parts now appeared on my left hind leg. Gone was the ugly protrusion and all seemed to be well with the world.

Soon I was led into another room where the folks were eagerly waiting to greet me. You would have thought that I was their young twenty-year-old son returning from the Battle of Gettysburg. They were hugging and kissing me and all the time trying to be careful not to bump up against the stitching on my hind leg. With those same tears in their eyes— my guess is they hadn't dried since the two of them were informed of the need for surgery—they slob-bered over me until the vet finally started talking to them. He thought the surgery went very well. The lump would be sent into the lab for analysis and in the meantime I should go home and just take it easy.

At this point the vet motioned for his assistant to grab something from the back room. Shortly she came back with this contraption that to this day is hard for me to describe, but is one I shall never forget. It was a pliable piece of plastic in the form of a cone. Before I could register a complaint, the vet is positioning this stupid-looking device over my head, snapping it snugly in place around my neck. The thing fanned out so that it gave the appearance that I was wearing a megaphone attached around my neck. Sort of like Nipper, but instead of the handsome Terrier cocking his ear to listen to the megaphone, he is wearing the darn thing. I had become a coney dog and, for the life of me, I had no idea why.

Well, it turns out that I was not to be trusted. The vet explained to the folks that it was imperative that I leave my leg alone and not try to lick it. The cone around my neck was the ingenious device that some vet with way too much time on his hands devised to insure that dogs not lick a wound. Yeah, unless I had a tongue about two feet long, there was no way I was going to be able to get at that stitching. Mission accomplished.

Terrific, but did any of you ever try to maneuver around your house wearing a plastic cone that fanned out to a good foot-and-a-half in width? Imagine the humiliation the first time I tried to walk into my crate when we got home. Without turning my head I could do nothing but ram myself headlong into the front of the crate. One of the folks had to help me turn my head to allow me the simple pleasure of going into my crate to lie down and relax after such an eventful day, my first as a coney dog.

Thankfully my days as a coney dog didn't last forever. Within a couple weeks the three of us returned to the vet's office where the seamstress removed the stitches and explained to the folks that I could resume my normal routine. The good Doctor of Darning explained that all had gone well with the removal of the nasty lump and that the results from the lab proved to be negative, no apparent signs of the big "C." The folks should just keep an eye out for any recurrences. Not a problem with that directive. Not another day in my life passed without the folks giving me the morning once over, making sure no more "its" had shown up over night.

Now let me think. Is this going to end up in
the Atlantic or the Pacific?

Eighteen
ACROSS
THE GREAT DIVIDE

Mom and Dad always had this love for all things Western. Away from their button-downed careers, they liked to dress Western and, to my utter embarrassment, they even dressed me Western. Yeah, I had a cowboy hat that, on special occasions, they insisted I wear. Why a hat named after a bovine and a young person of the male persuasion would be appropriate for Yours Truly, I couldn't fathom. But I humored them. No boots, thankfully, just the hat.

Well, after ten years living in the Midwest, the time finally came. Like pioneers in some classic Western movie, we pointed our wagon to the West. I had to wonder: Had the folks fallen prey to some silly Steinbeckian notion of living off the fat of the land? Had someone actually convinced them that the grass was greener on the other side of the Missouri? As we crossed that great river, it was clear to me, anyway, that there was *nothing* greener about the grass out West. In fact I would call it brown, nowhere near green, the color I had always favored.

Still, there was something alluring about this new landscape that must have stirred up strong emotions in the folks. I had seen my share of hills in our travels around the Midwest, but these were different. These suckers looked like hills that had been inflated with a giant air pump. The knolls started out innocently enough as we made our way across the plains, but in time they rose so high in the sky that it became nearly impossible to tell where the hills ended and the clouds took over.

I received a quick geology lesson when I heard Mom remark to Dad something about how spectacular the mountains were. So that was what you called these over-developed hills; they were mountains. Some of them rose so high up that at first glance I would have sworn there was snow resting atop them. I knew this was a ridiculous thought on my part, it being August with an outside temperature in the eighties and our air conditioner running at full throttle. But once again, some mumbling from the front seat cleared up my confusion. Dad commented on how lovely the peaks of the mountains looked with a coat of snow still left over from last winter. At this point, I began to wonder where we were going, to a place where the snow stays on the ground year round?

Well, we were headed to live in the mountains, far from the green fields of my beloved Midwest. I will admit to being more than a bit apprehensive about the move, but at ten years old I wasn't about to put my paw down and refuse to follow the folks out West.

Life soon settled into a routine not that different from back home. Dad was gainfully employed at the local university and Mom carried on as a member of the mobile workforce for the same company. I had grown quite comfortable in our Midwestern house in the country and was relieved to find we would be living outside the city limits out West.

Yes, out beneath the stars. Unencumbered by the ways of city folk. Free to relieve oneself outside regardless of where oneself might find oneself. But this was an entirely different kind of country than the type I had grown accustomed to in the Midwest. Little did I know at the time what awaited me in our new home in the mountains.

I will never forget our first morning in the new digs. The three of us laced up our running shoes—okay, the two of them did—and we headed down the long gravel driveway from our house to the nearest road. Before we had gone very far, I saw "her" out of the corner of my eye. The instant she saw the three of us, she froze in the ditch just off the road. She had long grayish-brown fur that blended in naturally with the rough-hewn landscape. From my vantage point she appeared to be about the size of a German Shepard. In fact, once we got closer, she began to shuffle along with that same cautious gait characteristic of the police dog. As we approached her alongside the gravel road, her gait changed abruptly from shuffle mode to stalking mode. Back and forth. Back and forth. It was soon obvious that she fully intended to keep herself positioned between us and something she considered quite valuable behind her.

I can honestly say that this was one of those rare instances when I was glad that I was attached to the folks via my handy dandy, flashy red retractable leash. We eventually reached the point on the road where we were directly across from this wild creature now standing at attention in the ditch. It soon became clear why she was mimicking one of those guards outside Buckingham Palace. Directly behind her was a den. Peeping their beady little eyes from inside the den was a litter of pups. But these were no ordinary pups, at least not like any I had ever seen. Turns out these were coyote pups and Momma was bound and determined to see that no humans or any animals of the four-legged variety would come between her and her pups.

Well, we didn't hesitate in respecting Momma's wishes and moving quickly past her and her brood. For the next few weeks, the routine continued. Every time we jogged down the big hill, she waited for us. And each time, she stalked us, intent on guarding the den. That was never a problem. None of the three of us had any interest in tangling with her as she protected her pups.

I remember that first night after our encounter with Ms. Wily Coyote. I had just settled into my crate when the cries started. First they sounded like they were far off in the distance. Then they became louder and more shrill. The mother coyote was calling out in the dark of the night. This was the most blood-curdling, primeval cry I had ever heard from another living being. Her howling was enough to keep me awake for some time. All sorts of questions started racing through my mind. *Why* was she calling out? And to *whom* were her cries directed? Then there was the question that really haunted me as I laid in the comfort of my crate listening to her. Was this a cry of anguish or one of elation? I don't recall now how long it took, but eventually I dozed off at the end of my first night in coyote country.

Come to find out these weren't the only four-legged creatures with whom we shared our property. One morning in early winter of that first year in our new home I was awakened by the sound of hoofs tromping through the yard just outside my window. I sauntered over to the window and put my front paws up on the ledge to get a peek at what the latest addition to our own personal version of the San Diego Zoo might be.

What I saw was enough to make you stand and take notice. I had seen plenty of deer back in the Midwest. Midgets compared to these monstrosities. These goliaths stood about ten feet tall and had some of the most impressive racks imaginable. Here they were just sauntering about in our yard as if they owned the place. The nerve of these guys.

The next thing I knew, one of them was making its way over to some very expensive trees we had just planted. Convenient for the critter, the trees were just about jaw level and he commenced to munching away. It was as if he just walked into one of those all-you-can-eat buffets and began helping himself. The only difference was that he hadn't bothered to pick up a plate and utensils and was eating all he wanted without returning to his seat. I thought to myself, *What a pig!* Hearing the folks talk about how much they had forked out for our spendy landscape job, I began barking at the top of my lungs to get the attention of either Mom or Dad. Both of them came running as I pressed my nose up against the windowpane.

I looked at the folks for some signal, my eyes as big as saucers. Did they want me to charge out the front door and see if I couldn't send the whole pack of them scattering in all directions? No, instead the folks just stood there with mouths wide open and a look in their eyes of sheer amazement. It turned out that our area was designated as an elk refuge. "Wapiti" was the name given to these wonders of nature by the Native Americans. Whatever you wanted to call them, they were the essence of class and style, walking around our front yard with the grace of young ballerinas. And, with winter settling in, these magnificent creatures had made their way down from the high country for the next few months.

After the initial shock wore off, I did warm up to the elk. The bulls had an air of nobility about them, holding those massive racks up high and tiptoeing along with such elegance. It was a real hoot to watch them face off against each other. Whether they were playing or really fighting, I never quite figured out. Two of them would start towards each other from just a few feet apart and then ram their gangly headgear into their opponent. Then, like sumo wrestlers, they stood frozen in position, pushing hard against the other until finally one of them backed off. I got such a kick out of watching them, of course safe within the confines of our house.

Now a chorus had been added to the melody of the coyotes howling at night. As I lie awake in my crate at night, I could hear the elk bugling off in the distance. Had this been the sound of car horns in the big city I doubt I would have been able to fall asleep at all, the racket these creatures made most nights. But there was something soothing, in a very natural way, about the howling of the coyotes and the bugling of the wapiti that made me sleep like a baby in our home in the mountains.

My adventures out West weren't limited to the wildlife out our front door. One of my most memorable experiences took place when Mom was out of town on one of her business trips. Turns out Dad had been asked to give a lecture in another city about three hours away, on the other side of the mountains. The trip would require him to stay overnight. But what would he do with "the dog"? Lucky me. The decision was made that I should accompany Pops on this little junket. I guess the folks figured I would be good company for him.

The ride over to the site of Dad's lecture was uneventful. We drove over in the late afternoon and watched the sun slowly set over the western horizon. It was early spring and the mountains were in full splendor, colorful blossoms dotting the rocky slopes. The time went by quickly and before I knew it we had reached our destination. Because Dad's lecture wasn't until the following evening, Mom had booked us in at one of those pet-friendly hotels, naturally requesting a no-smoking room.

The day of the lecture started out with a phone call to our room. The voice on the other end asked if Dad would be willing to come into the local TV station for a brief interview to be aired later on the evening news. So we drove to the station and, to my dismay, Dad left me in the Sit Up Vertically. Why wouldn't he want to show me off to all of the locals tuning in to their five o'clock news hour? Did he think I would embarrass him? At any rate I wasn't invited in and I waited patiently for Dad's return.

On his return we drove back to the hotel, freshened up, checked out, and drove to the local country club for a dinner hosted by the folks putting on the lecture. Again, I was left outside. From there it was off to the lecture and again, I was asked to wait outside. I was starting to get used to this treatment and decided that it was nothing personal. I would have thought Dad might have needed an assistant. You know, someone to click on the next PowerPoint slide when the presenter says, "Next slide, please." No such luck, so I took a nap and waited for Dad to return.

As I recall it was about nine o'clock when Pops returned from his lecture, appearing quite happy with himself for a job well done. He started up the Sit Up Vertically and we headed for home. But within minutes the weather took a turn for the worse, snow starting to fall at an ever-increasing pace. Now Dad had a decision to make. Should we plow forward and hope for the best or turn back and play it safe? The problem was that Dad had a class the next morning. He never missed a scheduled class. To him, canceling a class was unthinkable. We marched onward.

At this point I should mention something about the road. We weren't just cruising home on some flat Midwestern interstate, but rather we were headed up and over the Continental Divide on a two-lane highway. If you aren't familiar with the geographical significance of the divide, let me explain it to you as it was related to me by a male acquaintance of my species. Say you are standing high up in the mountains on the Continental Divide with your head facing due north. You lift your right leg to take a tinkle. As unfathomable as it may seem, that little dribble of yours will eventually find its way down a series of rivers and streams and end up in the Atlantic Ocean. Okay, now assume you want to prove your dexterity. You lift your left leg this time. Miraculously, your little contribution to the world's H_2O will someday end up in the Pacific Ocean. Amazing beyond belief, wouldn't you say?

Forgive me the babbling, but I have a hard time telling the story of our trip across the divide without a bit of diversion, frightening as this excursion turned out to be. So here are Dad and Yours Truly headed across the Great Divide to the other side. In a blinding snowstorm. Because we were in the mountains there was no radio or cell phone reception. We had lost contact with the outside world.

Occasionally, Dad looked up into the rearview mirror and tried to reassure me. "How you holding up back there, buddy? Shouldn't be too much longer till we drive out of this." The crack in his voice told me he didn't necessarily believe his own words.

Other than Dad's voice, there was nothing else

to break the silence except the wind howling out my window. We drove on at a snail's pace, at a speed you might expect from one of those overweight Basset Hounds. Every so often I looked up from my reclining position in the back of the Sit Up Vertically. This was one of the very few times I was horizontal in the back of the Sit Up Vertically, too terrified to look up for any period of time. Each time I got up enough nerve to look out, I saw nothing but blinding snow. A total whiteout. Thankfully the visibility was so poor you couldn't see the mile drop-off to the canyon floor, which I instinctively knew was down below us.

All sorts of thoughts run through your head at times like these. Here I was, a thirteen-year-old canine with my better years behind me. I barely survived my first year on this earth, me the terra dog. But once I did make it through that first year, I had quite a run. Literally and figuratively. Some dogs never leave the confines of their homes. Not me. I had traveled the highways and byways of this great land, always under the watchful eye of my adoring folks. If this was to be the end, then so be it. At least I would go down with one of them at my side. But what nonsense. What would become of Mom? How could she carry on without the two of us? I might be approaching the pearly gates, but I decided I wasn't ready to knock, not just yet. I had to keep a stiff upper lip and put my trust in Dad's ability to get us out of this predicament.

We must have driven for two hours in this whiteout. Eventually we reached a small town on the other side of the divide, the snow blowing so wildly the whole time I had no sense of when we had actually crossed over. By this time it was well past midnight. Dad got out to stretch and then disappeared into a bar, the only sign of life in this tiny outpost of civilization. I am guessing he just needed to relieve himself, but I wouldn't have blamed him if once inside he had asked the bartender for a straight shot of Jack Daniels. He wasn't gone long and I didn't smell any suspicion on him when he returned and lifted the back gate to check on me.

"Hey, Duff, we made it," he said as he scratched me behind both ears, his hands still shaky and his voice a bit crackly from our white-knuckle drive. I looked up from my reclining position, gave him a peck on the cheek, my show of thanks for keeping us alive. He returned my affection with a pat on the head and slowly closed the gate. We were going home.

As we headed down the highway the skies had cleared. The snow was still coming down, but vertically rather than horizontally as it had during the height of the storm. By the time we reached home, the snow had stopped altogether and the evening had turned tranquil. Every constellation in the universe was on display in the magnificent blue sky above us, a full moon illuminating the mountains off to the west. Three in the morning and we were finally home. I slept the rest of the night like a baby, thankful to have survived our trip across the Great Divide.

Nineteen

COMING CLEAN
(HEAVEN)

I was beginning to feel pretty good about my tale, not that far from wrapping it up, at least in my mind. This personal assessment may have been what caused me to step out of character and take the initiative for a change with Rex, Super Agent.

I had just polished off a rawhide on another glorious morning in Eden. I spotted Rex lying under the shade of an old oak tree just down the road. Out of habit this lovely spot had become our daily meeting place. As I trotted over to greet him, I cleared my throat just a bit, careful not to startle him, but at the same time giving no credence to that old adage, best to let sleeping dogs lie.

"Top of the morning to you, Rex. Hope I didn't

disturb you."

"Good morning to you, Duff. No, not at all. I guess I must have dozed off for a few minutes."

"Well, I survived that harrowing drive up and over the Great Divide and am now heading for home."

"Sorry, Duff," Rex replied, still sounding a bit groggy, "but I'm not sure what drive and what divide you are talking about."

"No, Rex, I am the one who should apologize. It is just that I am so excited about my tale—you know the T-A-L-E one—that I got a bit carried away. I am sure you remember me telling you about our move out West and the trip with Dad in a blinding snowstorm over the Continental Divide. Well, with the telling of that story I'm reaching the end of my tale—and I'm not talking about the stub on my back side."

It must have sounded to Rex like I had just downed a double espresso, wired as I was on this particular morning. "Terrific, Duff. That is great. I am delighted that you are getting your story written down," Rex said, looking at the ground in front of him.

This was the first occasion I could recall him not looking directly into my eyes as he spoke.

"Rex, forgive me for saying this, but I sense that you don't quite share my enthusiasm for the progress of my story. Is there something bothering you, my friend?"

"It's just that you seem to be forgetting one key ingredient. You may be getting your story written, but we are no closer to finding a publisher than we were the day you started writing. Out of the hundreds of queries I have made, the sole response was from the smart aleck who suggested that she and I do lunch. And do you recall what she wanted?"

"I sure do. I don't remember the details but it had something to do with me being a third dog, and acting like I was a human, rather than who I am, a dog. Is that who you are talking about?"

"That's the gal, alright. And you made it clear to me that this was your story to tell and you had no interest in taking on some other persona. I assume your position on this matter hasn't changed?"

"No, it hasn't, Rex. Indeed, it hasn't."

We both grew quiet. The only sound now was a gentle breeze rustling through the leaves on the big oak tree. Both of us stared off into the distance, neither one sure what more there was to say. I had a tale to tell but no way to get it back to Earth to the two people who most desperately needed to hear it.

I was beginning to feel a bit guilty about not contributing my fair share to the communal system,

Rex's occasional reminder that I someday would be able to donate my royalties notwithstanding. And speaking of donations, I had been pondering the notion that it might be nice to make a contribution to shelters that give my kind a chance. Granted, the last thing I needed up here was a tax deduction, but that wasn't the point. This would just be my way of giving back.

As we both stared off into space, I kept thinking back to Rex's uncanny knowledge of the publishing business. Just maybe he had a trump card up his sleeve, one that he was reluctant to play, but one that might be our meal ticket, our entrée into the world of editors. Finally, I broke the silence. "Do you remember the day we met, when I told you I wanted to get my story to my folks?"

"Of course I do. I was the one who encouraged you to expand your horizons, to put the whole story into a book, to be shared by everyone, not just your people."

"Yes, you were the one, Rex. You taught me about agents and editors, fact and fiction, persons and points of view. You opened my eyes to a whole new world. And do you recall me asking you that day how you knew so much about the publishing business?"

"I do, although I don't recall my exact response." The edge in Rex's voice indicated that he wasn't necessarily enjoying my third-degree interrogation.

"Well, I do remember it. You told me 'I have always been intrigued by the literary world and it certainly didn't hurt to be raised in the business. But that is for another day.' Those were your exact words. Well, Rex, it *is* another day."

Suddenly taken back a bit by my own candor, I shut up and listened for Rex's response. But there was none. He had turned away from me and was looking off into the endless horizon. Though I had come to understand that it was the only form of time up here, it seemed an eternity before Rex finally began to speak. And it was with a softness that I had never heard before in his voice.

"Fine. I might as well come clean, old chap. I was indeed raised in the publishing business. From the day he brought me home from the breeder I was immersed in all things literary. At the time he was a young sales rep for Hopkinton House, fresh out of college and just learning the business. He spent most of his time on the road, driving from one account to another, and he took me everywhere with him. When calling on a bookstore, he took great delight in introducing his 'associate,' as he called me. His standard joke with customers was that I never got the memo about 'business casual,' always dressed as I was in my black-and-white tux. We became the dynamic duo, the superstar salesman and his able sidekick. After two years he was promoted to editor, his first desk job, and guess who got a job under the desk? Yours Truly. I was the hit of the office, the great stress reliever for his colleagues tied to their cubicles day after day."

At this Rex paused, no doubt needing to catch his breath after such an outpouring. It wasn't hard to figure out that "he" was his adopted dad, but it seemed peculiar that Rex should refer to him with such an impersonal pronoun. I tried to tread softly.

"What a wonderful life the two of you must have had. Your dad was such a young man when you first met. I assume that your case was similar to mine, him outliving you. Was he still working in the business when you died?"

"I have no idea."

"I don't follow you. What do you mean you have no idea?"

"Just that. There is more to the story, Duff. The colleague in the next cubicle over from ours happened to be a petite young blonde with baby-blue eyes. She oohed and aahed over me like all the others but I had my suspicions about a possible ulterior motive. I eventually came to the conclusion that she saw me as a convenient conduit to him. And what a conduit

I became. Before long the two of them became the talk around the water cooler, the handsome young editor and the perky blonde in the next cubicle over. I tried to set aside any petty jealousy, seeing how his eyes lit up whenever she stuck her head around the corner. Only problem was, every time she did, she started sneezing. Incessantly, nonstop. He handed her a Kleenex but the sneezing wouldn't stop until she retreated to her own cubicle. Before long it was obvious that she was allergic to dogs."

Now Rex had my undivided attention with his gripping story of office romance. "So, what happened, Rex? I assume he eventually had to break it off with her, the two of you being so inseparable?"

"Life doesn't always work out the way you assume it will, old chap. I will spare you the details. He proposed to her and she had one condition on accepting his proposal."

"You're kidding, aren't you, buddy?"

"I wish I were. He had tears in his eyes the day he loaded me in his car for the long drive. He told me this was the hardest thing he ever had to do. But the boy was hopelessly in love. I may not have made my grand arrival in a squad car as you did, but like you I found myself a guardian of the state so to speak, a Pound Hound, or in my case a Shelter Terrier. So after three years together, that was it. My days in the publishing business were over."

Again, Rex grew silent. As much as I knew he would rather not go further, I couldn't let him stop mid-story. Tiptoeing like a trapeze artist on a tight-rope, I continued. "So, Rex, I just knew we had a common bond. I may have been a country boy and you a city gentleman, but isn't it amazing we both landed in shelters? We are part of that great fraternity of abandoned animals that knows what it is like to go from feeling unloved to eventually finding someone who will take you in and love you the rest of your life. I am just curious, buddy, did it take as long in the shelter to find someone to adopt you as it did me? How long were you there?"

"About twelve hours."

"I must not have heard you correctly. Did you mean twelve weeks or twelve months?"

"No, I meant just what I said, about twelve hours. He brought me to the shelter in the morning and they put me in a temporary holding pen. Only problem was no one noticed that the window in the room was left unlocked. As soon as it turned dark I nudged it open with my nose, jumped out, and ran for my life. From that moment on, I lived on the streets of Boston until the day I died at the ripe old age of sixteen."

Curious as I was to know what life was like on the streets of Boston for all those years, I knew the limits. I felt guilty for pressing as hard as I had, with my own ulterior motive of hoping Rex still had some contacts in the business who might be able to help us.

"I'm sorry, old pal. I had no idea."

"That's okay. If you will excuse me now, I would rather be alone." With that, Rex turned and walked away slowly, the only time I had ever seen him without a trot in his gait.

Without a word said between us, we both found ourselves under that big oak tree every morning about the same time, like two old codgers meeting up for coffee. Rex was usually under the shade of the tree first, but on the morning after his coming clean there was no sign of him as I trotted up. Instead, I found an envelope wedged between two low-lying branches of the tree. The paw writing on the front of the envelope read:

Good morning, Duff. You know better than anyone that we all have stories to tell. We just need someone to listen to them. Until yesterday, I didn't want to tell my story, but the Bulldog in your breeding brought out my tale of woe and for that I thank you. Now we must move on and get your tale out there. I don't want to get your hopes up, but enclosed is a fresh start.

Rex had a way to put you on the edge of your seat, even if that seat was nothing more than a patch of grass under an oak tree. I tore open the envelope and began reading.

Bradley Wellington
Hopkinton House
444 East Galaxy Drive
Boston, MA
Dear Mr. Wellington:
    Maybe when you were growing up your family owned a dog. Or, possibly later in life you had a dog of your own, or for that matter maybe you still do. Even if you have never owned a dog, perhaps you have visited the local shelter or provided financial support for those wonderful creatures awaiting adoption.
    Let's face it. Our society is infatuated with our four-legged friends and nowhere is this phenomenon more in evidence than in the literary world. With that in mind, I enclose for your consideration my client's nearly completed, riveting story, Duffy: The Tale of a Terrier.
    My client has chosen to tell the story of a rescue dog in the first person, but instead of his own voice he uses that of the dog. It was only after Duffy moves on to the afterlife that he begins to put his

thoughts on paper, with the encouragement of his buddy, a literary easterner of the Boston Terrier persuasion named Rex. Granted this unique point of view introduces a bit of fantasy into the story, but isn't there something whimsical anyway about the unconditional bond that exists between people and their pets?

After a rough start, Duffy is rescued from a shelter and spends the remaining thirteen years of his life doing everything within his power to please his adopted parents. The Terrier mix travels the country with them and experiences life as few dogs are fortunate enough to do.

I would much prefer that you spend your valuable time reading from Duffy: The Tale of a Terrier *rather than listening to the ramblings of some agent, so with that I close and say that I look forward to hearing from you soon and sharing Duffy's complete tale. Regards,*

R. Terrence Bostwick III

rtbostwick3@hvmail.com

I folded the letter and stuck it back in the envelope. The sun was just beginning to come up over the horizon and the big oak tree provided a perfect spot to watch another glorious sunrise and then maybe fade into a morning nap. But no nap for me, not on this day. I had a tale to finish telling and an agent who had enough faith in me that he was willing to play his one remaining trump card just to try to sell my story.

Everyone always marvels at the incredibly
heightened sense of smell dogs have.
And this is a *good* thing?

Twenty

THE TEN BEST (AND WORST) THINGS ABOUT BEING A DOG

After the harrowing ride over the Great Divide, I was more content than ever to spend my evenings curled up in our living room, watching a little TV with the folks. Like all house dogs, I saw my share of television over the years. Don't let any dog try and tell you he never watched. If he does, he is just trying to be highbrow, as if he is too intellectual for something as crass as the boob tube. All dogs like TV. I suppose before long they will come up with a reality show for dogs. You know, a day in the life of FIDO, that sort of thing.

Anyway, when the folks allowed me to, I enjoyed staying up for a bit of late-night TV. Let's face it.

Most of us are either Leno or Letterman guys. You choose. Myself, I always favored Dave. Maybe it had something to do with the stupid pet tricks.

Before I finish my tale, I thought it would be nice to give you an insider's look at what makes a dog happy, and at times, maybe not so happy. So, with a nod to Letterman, here is my list of the ten best (and worst) things about being a dog.

10: (BEST) WE NEVER HAVE TO WORRY ABOUT WHAT TO WEAR.

All that time humans spend buying clothes. And then every day stare mindlessly into a closet, trying to decide what to wear that day. Now, let's see, will it be the blue slacks with the camel hair jacket? No wait, something more casual, the green polo shirt with the khakis? What nonsense. Can you imagine the time that would be freed up for the important things in life—i.e., sleeping and eating—if you just went au naturel every day?

(WORST) WE NEVER GET TO WORRY ABOUT WHAT TO WEAR.

Sure, what a pleasure in those warm summer months to wake up, stretch, and trot out the door without giving a thought to the weather. But on the other hand...can you imagine what it is like heading outside in the dead of winter, wearing nothing but a smile? Let's just say that smile doesn't stick around very long and that you learn to take care of your business in pretty short order and then make a beeline back inside to curl up on your favorite pillow next to a roaring fire. Incidentally, where does "taking care of business" come from, anyway? What a weird expression for something that has absolutely nothing to do with commerce, making a living, or anything of the sort. Don't get me started, don't *even* get me started.

I must admit that every so often I ended up in something other than just my birthday suit—now there is one of those expressions humans have that actually *does* make sense—the suit I was born in and the suit I wear every day. Like the time my aunt sent me a "bones" outfit for Halloween. The aunt's husband was a doctor and she ran his office. So what costume do I get? A black-and-white skeleton! I certainly had the perfect body for it. And then there was my ski parka. The folks figured that with my extra-short hair, I needed this for the cold weather. The coolest thing about the parka was the stylish colors. Every color of the rainbow.

DUFFY

9: (BEST) WE GET TO GO OUTSIDE TO GO.

Picture this: No waiting in long lines at sporting events. Although it isn't that often we dogs are allowed at such events, unless it is one of those rare occasions where some baseball team invites ticket holders to bring their dogs along to the park. You know, one of those cutesy promotional gimmicks they might call Bark at the Park or a Day with Babe Woof. No having to hold it through a movie for us. Forget having to cross your legs until they turn blue because you can't find a rest stop along the interstate. You need to go, you just notify your folks, they open the door, and out you trot. Not to get too philosophical about it, but for my money nothing beats the pleasure you feel as you tinkle, gazing up at the Big Dipper and a full moon. Okay, just admit it, all of you guys know what I am talking about here. Sure, for us male canines there is the necessity of finding a tree, a wall, or some suitable facsimile to "mark," but, hey, it isn't that hard to improvise.

(WORST) WE HAVE TO GO OUTSIDE TO GO.

As I mentioned earlier, our Midwestern house in the country was perfectly set up for me to take a quick squirt, my dog run jutting out conveniently on the back side of the house. Still, we lived in a part of the country where on a cold wintry night the temperature often dipped below zero. This is one of those very few areas where cats have it over us. Say Garfield needs to relieve himself. No big deal, he just saunters over to the litter box. No such luck for a dog on one of those nights when the windchill is twenty below and you have to pee like a racehorse. Believe me, you learn in a hurry not to tarry. You do what needs to be done and bolt back inside to the warmth of the house as quickly as you can.

8: (BEST) WE GET TO EAT THE SAME CHOW EVERY DAY.

At least some dogs do, those that live the type of privileged life that I did. Nothing but the best for their boy, thought my folks. I ate the top-of-the-line chow from that first day home.

And then there is the hassle factor. No worrying about what to wear or what's for din-din. Think of all the time that humans could save here. For example, how much time do they waste trying to decide what to fix for dinner? All that time blown cruising up and down the aisles at the local market. Or you go out to a swank restaurant and the menu is so heavy you need two hands to hold it up. "How is your salmon prepared this evening? Can you recommend a nice

Pinot Grigio to go with it?" *Give me a break*. The time humans blow over something as basic as eating is comical to me. No such dilemma for a dog. Come seven in the morning and six at night, the folks slide the same chow in front of you. You inhale it without as much as a pause, lap up a bit of water—no need for bottled; tap is just fine—and trot off for a nap.

(WORST) WE EAT THE SAME CHOW EVERY DAY.

Now believe me, I am not complaining too loudly here. What could be so bad about dog food that costs thirty bucks for a forty-pound bag? But still, day after day after day? It would have been nice if every so often the folks would have switched it up just a tiny bit. Maybe throw in an occasional table scrap with the yuppie puppy food. But the closest I ever got to anything different in my bowl was an occasional pill for my allergies. I learned in a hurry, though, that pills are not delicacies and I just ate around them.

7: (BEST) WE GET TO GO WEEKS BETWEEN BATHS.

Depending on your coat and personal hygiene habits, most dogs do go for weeks at a time without a bath. As I have described, I was a short-haired Terrier. Like your basic white Chevy, my light-colored coat never really showed the dirt much. I always pitied those Black Labs, knowing how difficult it was for them to stay clean. On the other hand, I was what Mom often described as a wash-and-wear dog. Well, much of that washing was personally administered. Once the folks went off to bed, I often gave myself a good licking. It is amazing what a dog can do with a little saliva and a limber tongue, as everyone knows we are capable of reaching places humans could never reach. Think of how often you have marveled about the ability of a pooch to reach those old private parts.

Personal hygiene is another one of those areas in which humans seem to waste an inordinate amount of time and money. I've heard that some even build lavish rooms in their houses for the sole purpose of rinsing themselves off. Spas, Jacuzzis, hot tubs, such extravagance.

If you are a lucky dog, the folks only subject you to a bath every few months, or maybe slightly more frequently if you have rolled in something ripe. My folks didn't humiliate me by plopping me down in some corrugated steel tub in the laundry room. No, I went to a groomer and spent the day at the spa. My personal groomer gave me a good thorough bathing, clipped my toenails, checked the glands, and sent me off with a biscuit. What could be so bad?

DUFFY

(WORST) WE HAVE TO GO WEEKS BETWEEN BATHS.

This is another one of those areas where you would like to be able to choose your spots, maybe compromise once in awhile. Say you have just come in the house after a long day of chasing rabbits. Every muscle in your body aches from the all-out strain of the hunt. How nice it would be to take a soak in the tub just like humans do. Just a few minutes to soothe those aching muscles and you would be ready for another day. And have you ever noticed a dog with one of those itches that just won't seem to go away? When you scratch behind his ear you would think that he is experiencing a sensation from another world. An occasional bath would certainly help out here.

6: (BEST) WE HAVE AN INCREDIBLE SENSE OF SMELL.

As you are no doubt aware, canines have a sense of smell second to none. A rabbit could be hiding in a bush a hundred yards away and we are going to know it. As another example, say Elmer next door is grilling T-bones on the Weber. With a nose like mine, you can almost taste them. Believe me, there is nothing more tantalizing to a dog, even though you know that none of that wonderful red meat will ever reach your mouth.

TEN BEST (& WORST) THINGS ABOUT BEING A DOG

(WORST) BOY, DO WE HAVE AN INCREDIBLE SENSE OF SMELL.

Sure, most of those smells like the T-bones are well worth sniffing. But like everything in life, there are exceptions. Imagine Pepé Le Pew is just crossing the road up ahead. Before humans pick up that horrible scent it has long since reached our nostrils. As another case in point, and I will try to put this as delicately as I know how, say someone in a crowded room passes a bit of gas. Take my word for it, we four-legged guys know about it far in advance of any humans. Just admit it. You have probably been guilty a time or two of the sorriest excuse in the book: Oh, the dog did it.

5: (BEST) WE CAN HEAR ANYTHING AND EVERYTHING.

Just like our sniffers, dogs are born with an incredible set of ears. And I am not talking about the sheer size of them, like the ones you see on one of those forlorn-looking Bassett Hounds, the sidekick to the Maytag repairman. I am referring to the fact that our ears pick up every sound nature has to offer. The melody of robins chirping in the springtime. Or the sounds of water washing along the shore. When you are a dog, every one of these pleasant sounds is magnified.

DUFFY

(WORST) WE HEAR ANYTHING AND EVERYTHING.

Early on in my time with the folks, it became apparent that I would be allowed to go just about everywhere with them. We went to the grocery store. We went to the bank, which, by the way, was almost always good for a biscuit if I put a pitiful enough look on my face for the teller at the drive-through window. It didn't matter where they went, the folks just liked having me along.

So it was only natural that first year in my new home for them to take me to the Fourth of July parade. Big mistake. We all found out in a hurry that this was no place for me. Imagine yourself in the front row of a heavy metal concert. This is what it sounds like to a dog when the sirens start going off, when the high school marching bands start blaring out of key, and when those middle-aged men in the funny-looking hats come riding their magic carpets down the street, blowing their whistles. I thought my delicate little ear drums were going to pop at my first parade. I made it perfectly clear with some well-placed whimpering that I had no interest in this sort of spectacle.

4: (BEST) WE CAN FALL ASLEEP
AT THE DROP OF A HAT.

No need for sleeping pills for dogs. All those ads on television telling you what you need to take to get that good night's sleep. Only problem is that the list of possible side effects is usually a mile long. Oh sure, this pill will help you fall asleep, but when you wake up you may have permanent brain damage. No thanks. Let me make a suggestion. Don't go to bed worrying about that next payment on the yacht, whether Junior will get into Yale, or whether you will get that big promotion. No wonder you can't sleep. Chill out and next thing you know you will be sleeping like a baby, or better yet, like a dog.

By the way, our ability to fall asleep at the drop of a hat is shared by most of our animal friends. Did you know that most horses sleep standing up? It seems crazy to me. Why you wouldn't want to plop down on your belly to sleep is beyond me but, hey, that is what makes horse racing.

(WORST) WE SLEEP AWAY THREE-FOURTHS
OF OUR LIVES.

Looking back, I wonder what all I missed in those hours I napped. It is one thing to sleep through the night, because everyone else in the house is also sawing logs. But what *did* I miss sleeping so much? The life of a dog is short enough as it is, so it is a shame that I dozed through three-fourths of mine. Oh well, life, however short or long, is full of tradeoffs.

3: (BEST) WE DON'T HAVE TO ENGAGE IN MEANINGLESS CONVERSATIONS.

Say you are at some fancy dinner party with the folks. Boring as the couple standing next to them may be, simple etiquette requires that the folks act interested in the latest soccer exploits of Billy or what the newest research has to say about potty training. As a dog, no such expectations exist. No one expects you to say anything, so you can just sit there grinning and never say a word.

(WORST) WE HAVE A VERY LIMITED VOCABULARY.

There certainly are times when it would be nice to speak up. It's like no one ever asks your opinion. Well, they do, but then it isn't like they expect you to respond. Sure, I learned to respond to questions the folks put to me with a good old wag of the tail, what little I had. "Would you like to go for a ride, Duff?" A quick wag told them all they needed to know. But on the other hand, what if they asked *where* I might want to go? No, for that one I never had much of an answer.

TEN BEST (& WORST) THINGS ABOUT BEING A DOG

2: (BEST) WE GET TO WALK AROUND ON FOUR LEGS.

Think of how much more coordinated you would be if you could use all four appendages for balance! Have you ever seen a dog slip on the ice? Of course not. And take digging. Think of how much easier it is when you can brace yourself with your back legs and then shovel away with the front ones. What do you mean, you don't dig? Where do you bury bones that you want to save for later?

(WORST) WE HAVE TO WALK AROUND ON FOUR LEGS.

Sure, dogs do have a bird's-eye view of everything at floor level, but when you are on all fours it makes it hard to see the food on the kitchen counter, unless you either jump up or happen to be a Great Dane. No question about it, being vertically challenged presents its obstacles.

AND THE NUMBER 1 BEST THING ABOUT BEING A DOG:

(BEST) WE PACK A LOT INTO EVERY DAY OF OUR LIVES.

Why do you think it is that dogs sleep so much? Every waking hour is spent chewing on rawhides, playing with pull ropes, and chasing after Frisbees. And, of course, doing whatever it takes to please the folks. They want to scratch your belly, you obligingly roll over and let them have at it. They want to take you for a run through the park, you don't refuse. You live for the moment.

(WORST) WE HAVE TO PACK A LOT INTO EVERY DAY.

We all know the statistics here. The average life span of my species is a fraction of what it is for our two-legged companions. Horses and even those dreaded cats usually live longer than dogs. How would you like it if they told you that you likely wouldn't live much more than twelve or fourteen years, maybe even less if you were one of those purebreds? Maybe dogs aren't really aware of this stark reality, but you would sure think we are the way we lead our lives, living as if every day might be our last.

**When someone asks a dog to act his age,
do they mean in dog years or human years?**

Twenty-one

THAT AGE-OLD QUESTION: WAS I FOURTEEN OR 5,120?

Where was I? Oh, yes, I was talking about the average life span of dogs. Not that I ever gave much thought to such things during my life. What in the world is this preoccupation most people seem to have with age? Isn't it just a number?

Take, for example, my age as humans would figure. As best as I can recall, I had my fourteenth birthday about a month before I "moved on." I know you would normally say "passed on," but that sounds creepy—let's go with "moved on."

Now you may be wondering: If I was adopted, how did my folks know my exact birthday? Let's just say that they used some creative accounting to come up with one for me. You see, I was adopted on September 22. The people at the shelter thought that I was about eight months old at that time. So the folks just counted backwards and figured my birthday was January 22. I went along with it, knowing that they got a kick out of celebrating my "birthday." What the heck, it was usually good for at least an extra rawhide if not something even more exotic like a pig's hoof.

But I digress. Humans do the craziest things with numbers. Like saying that I lived to be fourteen in "dog years." What else would you call them? When Uncle Otto dies when he is eighty, does his obituary read that he lived to be eighty in "human years?"

But take my moving on as an example. You should have heard all of the jabber after I left. "Oh, that Duffy, he had a good life. You know he lived to be almost 100 in human years!" All of the math geeks pulled out their pocket calculators, multiplied seven times fourteen, and decided that I was the equivalent of ninety-eight years old.

Who came up with the crazy notion that a dog year is equivalent to seven human years anyway? Granted, dogs have a way of packing more fun into one year than most humans are able to in seven years, but still!

Allow me to digress further. Who came up with

the silly idea of measuring one's age in years? Again, I was allegedly fourteen at the time of my moving on. Couldn't you just as easily say that I was 5,120? Get the calculator out again. Assume 365 days in a year and take that number times my fourteen years. Add on another ten days for how long I lived after my fourteenth birthday and there you have it. I lived to be 5,120 days old. Yeah, I know we would probably need to adjust for a few leap years in there, but let's don't get too carried away! Better yet, just say I lived to be 5,120. Very impressive indeed.

Why stop there? Pull that calculator back out and let's figure out how old I was in hours. "That Duffy. He sure had a great life. Why, you know he lived to be 122,880!"

Why stop there? "You know the old boy didn't look too bad for someone in his 7,000,000s!" And then you hear someone say under their breath "minutes, that is."

Okay, enough is enough, you say. But, have I made my point? Why all the hang-up with numbers and ages? If I were ever called upon to give a commencement address—silly as it sounds, can you imagine how handsome I would look in a cap and gown—this would be my point. Forget about age. Why should that limit what we are able to accomplish in our lives?

Why should it stifle the amount of happiness we are able to pack into our time on this terra? Live every day to its fullest. Why stop there? Live every hour and every minute to its fullest. Better yet, forget all of the crap about time. Live, period.

Twenty-two

SAVE THE SAP
(HEAVEN)

After that memorable day when I found the envelope between the two branches of the big oak tree, I didn't see much of Rex. Occasionally we crossed paths walking from one cloud to the next, but whenever I saw him he appeared distracted and I thought it best to give him his space. So I was surprised—and in my prior life would have been tickled to death—when a few weeks later he came trotting up to our old meeting place, his bug eyes as buggy as ever and his teeth clenched down on a sheet of paper.

"Hello there, old chap," he greeted me in his customary manner.

"Rex, so good to see you again. Great morning to be a..." I caught myself, still getting used to this relatively new existence of mine.

Rex seemed in no mood for small talk as he dropped the piece of paper from his mouth and suggested I read for myself a response he had just received from none other than Bradley Wellington with Hopkinton House, Boston, Massachusetts. As if Rex had just deposited a filet mignon at my feet, I eagerly picked up the letter and began reading.

Dear Mr. Bostwick,

Thank you for your letter and the chapters from Duffy: The Tale of a Terrier. *As you suggest, many readers can relate to the joys of sharing life with a dog. I am one of those, owning a dog many years ago, before the realities of the life of an editor took hold (ironically, he was a Terrier with the same name as Duffy's make-believe friend). I agree with your assessment of the current popularity of dogs and that one must strike while the iron is hot.*

First, let me say that I am not in the least put off with the Terrier's voice. Dogs have long been given the power of speech in literature and such a perspective opens up the reader's imagination to a whole new world. Duffy's humorous take on life with his adopted parents is refreshing and makes for a delightful read.

Having sung the praises of your client's story, I must admit to one serious concern. When dealing with the bond between humans and their pets it is far too easy to become sentimental, especially with a story such as this one where the dog starts out in a shelter.

SAVE THE SAP (HEAVEN)

While I see nothing wrong with a bit of romanticism or a dose of nostalgia, sentimentality just doesn't sell. I have yet to see the story's ending, but your client is best advised to spare his readers the schmaltz. He should save the sap for making maple syrup. Corn makes good flakes, not good literature.

As an agent you are fully aware of the harsh realities of the publishing business. Our editorial board has become more fastidious in signing new projects than any time in the history of the press. Currently, nine out of ten projects that editors bring forward for consideration are rejected by the board. This being said, I would be willing to read a complete manuscript when your client has finished his story.

Sincerely,
Bradley Wellington
Hopkinton House

I sat the letter down and turned to Rex. "What do you make of this, Rex?"

"I make of it that Mr. Wellington has fond memories of his time with his dog, though I beg to differ that it was 'the realities of the life of an editor' that caused him to become an *ex*-dog owner. I don't have much faith in turning our fate over to some editorial board, but what other options do we have at this point? My advice to you is to wrap up that tale of yours. When you do, we'll ship it off to our Mr.

Wellington and put it in the hands of him and his editorial board."

"Sounds good to me, Rex. I'm out of here."

"Oh, and one more thing," Rex hollered out, a twinkle in his eye, "remember, with our apologies to Lassie and Old Yeller, be sure to save the sap."

**Mountains are nice to look at,
but the older you get nothing beats the green,
green fields of home.**

Twenty-three
THE GREEN FIELDS
OF HOME

So I was zeroing in on fourteen years old, or 5,000 days, take your pick.

After living about 1,000 of those days out West, the folks announced one day that we were moving back home. Don't take me too literally here. Not back to the same house. Or even the same city or the same state for that matter. But back to the Midwest. The place of my arrival into the world. Where I was adopted. Where I was altered. Where I received my formal education.

Looking back, I have to wonder what the real motivation was for our latest move. Surely there was more to it than that nail-biting ride Dad and I took over the Great Divide. I can't imagine that the coyotes and elk were driving us out. I actually looked forward to seeing these creatures of the wild roaming about the property.

Officially, our move had something to do with a new "job opportunity" for Dad. Humans have this tendency to justify their nomadic wanderings on the basis of economic considerations. But me, I think there was more to this relocation than met the eye. I really believe that the folks knew I was nearing the end of my race and that they would rather see me cross the finish line in the part of the country where I first sprung out of the starting blocks.

It was a bit strange at first, coming back home after those three years out West. I had grown fond of the mountains, just as long as I didn't have to cross over them in a blinding snowstorm again. But it didn't take me long to feel like I was home. We were back on the prairie, on the flatlands where the horizon stretched out forever. Fields of corn and soybeans and freshly mowed hay, Holsteins grazing in emerald pastures of grass, peacefully chewing their cud.

The thing I will always remember about arriving back in the Midwest was how lush everything appeared, especially after living in the arid West. We arrived in the late summer, when the land was still sporting its finest coat of green. The corn stood proudly at attention, shooting skyward in the brilliant sun. The sweet aroma of alfalfa filled the air.

It wasn't just the flora, but the fauna were different, too. No more coyotes howling at the moon. No more elk, although their smaller cousins, the deer, were abundant in the area where we moved. And plenty of rabbits and squirrels to be chased. Ah, yes, I remembered these formidable foes fondly from my early years.

The truth be told, I still had the chase in me, but the chances of me catching up to a rabbit or a squirrel were slim to none, and a heck of a lot closer to the latter than the former. Let's face it: I was slowing down. I had started to grow a little gray around the whiskers. Of course, I didn't need to worry about my hair turning white, as that was its natural color from birth.

We had been in the new house barely a month. I woke up one morning from a deep sleep to see both the folks carrying their suitcases down the hallway in one hand, clutching airline tickets in the other. Usually this was a not-so-subtle signal to me that I would be sent to "camp." But in the short time we had been at the new place no suitable kennel had yet been found for me, at least not one that I had been told about.

Turns out, Mom was being honored with a big dinner to celebrate her twenty-five years with the same company. You know, the gold watch, toasts being made, all that sort of stuff. I was naturally quite proud of her, but to my amazement I wasn't invited to the gala. The dinner was to take place out of state, back where Mom had spent most of that quarter century. Dad would go for the celebration, but he would need to be back for his classes the next day. So time was limited and they would need to fly. What to do with Duff? This was going to be such a short trip that it seemed a shame to pack me up for camp for such a brief stay.

Home Alone. You remember the movie. Only in this case it was Yours Truly being left behind. A first time for everything, I figured, even at my advanced age of fourteen. Still, when I saw both of the folks heading out the door with their suitcases, I began to wonder. How did they expect me to take care of my bodily functions, let alone get my meals on my own? I had heard of cats being left alone in houses with their litter boxes. Any dignified dog wouldn't think of relieving himself in a box, so what was the plan here, anyway?

Not to worry. As I should have expected, Mom had all of this arranged before taking off. She had enlisted the help of our neighbor to come and let me out, and feed me my supper that night, and breakfast the next morning. My new best friend was impressed by my good manners. But who wouldn't be on their best behavior around someone who would be seeing to your most basic needs? I apparently made quite an impression on my caregiver. On their return he told the folks that I had been "a little gentleman."

Well, as I started to say, the little gentleman was slowing down. By January of our first year back in the Midwest I spent most of my time sleeping. Except when I was summoned for our daily run. I may have lost a step or two, but I still never passed up the chance to get some fresh air. The folks could sense that I was moving slower, and so naturally they cut me some slack.

Mornings I was especially sluggish. Once I did get up I was good to go, but it took me awhile to get the old bones in motion. Naturally my sluggishness concerned the folks, and so after a few mornings of my stumbling around, it was off to the vet. Nothing jumped out from a routine physical. Maybe I was coming down with a bit of arthritis, an affliction not limited to homo sapiens, a malady that can affect animals as well. A daily dose of pills might help if in fact it was arthritis.

Life returned to normal for a couple of weeks. February was just around the corner and that meant another installment of Westminster. I could only hope this would be the year the mixed breeds would be allowed to compete for Best in Show.

Though it was the dead of winter, we still tried to get out as much as possible and stay active. We checked out all of the happenings in our new town. One of these seemed a bit strange to us newcomers. Each year the town sponsored a hot air balloon festival. In February. In the Midwest. Pardon the pun, but it did sound pretty cool to me, a bunch of colorful balloons, hot flames shooting out from under them, the balloons all the while circling overhead, high above the frozen tundra.

The folks had promised me that the following weekend we would all take in the spectacle of these magnificent balloons lighting up the arctic sky over our town. I was really looking forward to this event. Maybe we could even take a ride in one of these strange contraptions.

I woke up on Wednesday of that week and it was clear that I had something going on that was more than just a little soreness in the joints. I got up to hop out of my crate and I had no hop to me. No giddyup, and the last thing I felt was giddy. To make matters worse, my breathing was labored, as if I had just finished one of those 5Ks. I lay back down in my crate for a minute, thinking that whatever was bothering me would pass. I tried to get up a second time and once more the old wheels failed me. I continued to struggle with my breathing.

The folks were naturally freaking out. It was early morning and so a call was made to the ER. The vet on call said that they should bring me in right away. Mom put my parka on to protect me against a bitterly cold wind that morning. Normally I hopped into the back of the Sit Up Vertically of my own accord. This time Dad had to help me. A bit of a blow to my dogly pride, but what is an ailing dog to do? Off we went.

X-rays revealed the vet's worst suspicion. I wasn't moving well because a large nasty lump was getting in the way. No wonder I couldn't get a normal rhythm to my breathing. The ER vet described the gruesome details to the folks. I chose to focus on more pleasant thoughts like my yet-to-be-served breakfast.

By the time the folks hashed things over with the ER vet, our local vet's office was now open for business. So off we went again, this time with X-rays in hand. After some brief consultation with my primary care physician, everyone agreed—though I don't recall having a vote myself in this decision—that the only thing to do was put me under and try to remove as much of the tumor as possible.

The vet led me to the back room and told the folks to wait in the sitting room. After a few minutes I reappeared, hooked up to a bunch of tubes and dragging an IV bottle. The vet had brought me out to say both hello and goodbye to the folks. I did my best theatrics to try and convince Mom and Dad that the former greeting was more appropriate than the latter, but I don't know if I was very convincing. What a sight for sore eyes I must have been, dragging that bottle around like some patient on a daytime soap opera. Mom and Dad each gave me a peck on the old snout and promised to be back for me as soon as I recovered from the surgery.

As soon as the anesthesia took hold, I was out like a light. I fell into a deep sleep. The next thing I knew I was awake but very groggy from a tough surgery. Too soon to eat anything solid, I lapped up a bit of water. I slept pretty much the rest of the day and well into the night. In fact, that night was the deepest sleep I had ever experienced. And I had a whopper of a dream, one to rival my appearance all those years ago at the Westminster.

The balloon rises gently above a frozen field. From my perch in a wicker basket I look up to see the brightly colored balloon painted with pictures of every type of dog conceivable to man. Small dogs, large dogs. Short hairs, long hairs. Black dogs, white dogs, and every color in between. I look around but find that I am the only one on board. No folks, no vet, no pilot, just me. How am I supposed to direct this big bird sans wings? But soon I realize there is no need for a pilot.

The balloon is sailing effortlessly of its own volition above our town as I peer over the side of my basket to see what I am leaving behind. Snowflakes fall softly to the ground. Soon the whole world appears in focus below me. Not just our town, but the entire world. Something else strikes me as strange. This panorama of the world is not confined to a moment in time, but encompasses all of my fourteen years of life. The Terrier, the terra dog, the earth dog, is leaving planet Earth, the only home he has ever known.

I catch my breath and take another cautious peek over the side of the basket. Out of nowhere scenes are playing out below me, each one proceeding at its own pace and its own cadence, like separate rings at the circus. Even though it is the dead of winter, I am struck by the kaleidoscope of colors in this diorama unfolding beneath me. Every color of the rainbow.

I peer down to see a familiar-looking red barn. A big door leading into the second floor hayloft swings open. Out flies a young pup, his ears flupping in the breeze, his eyes wide open to whatever it might be that awaits him below. He appears frozen in mid-air.

I glance to my right and that same pup is being led down a long corridor of an animal shelter. In the next frame he bounces off a wall and on the rebound ends up in the laps of a young couple. The startled looks on their faces make it clear they aren't sure what to make of this lively Bull Terrier.

From here I bring into focus a picture straight out of suburbia. That same young pup reappears. In the backyard of a two-story frame house he scampers from one end of the yard to the other, chasing effortlessly after a ball his proud owner has thrown his way. A miniature barn sits against the back of the house. The owner motions the pup to come and check it out. The little guy peeks cautiously into the small opening of the dog house.

Soon my eyes are drawn to a frame in which the dog has started to fill out. He has lost some of his puppy fat and is wearing a bright shiny collar. His owners are putting him through his paces. The dog is learning to heel, to sit, to stay, to respond to each of the commands they give him.

Mimicking real life, the action accelerates, at what appears to be **seven** times the normal speed. It is as if someone hit the fast forward button on a DVR. The young Terrier's life is flashing before me at a rapid-fire pace.

A new house in the country. A fancy dog run built just for him.

Proud owners and an equally proud Terrier crossing the finish line at a dog walk.

Mountains with snow-covered peaks off in the horizon.

A coyote howling at a full moon just now appearing in the sky.

A herd of elk meandering across the frozen landscape.

In the final scene, the rugged terrain is replaced with a

THE GREEN FIELDS OF HOME

patchwork quilt of corn, oats, and soybeans.
Ah, the green fields of home, I think to myself.

Suddenly my balloon comes to a halt, although I don't really sense that I am on solid ground, a surface that has always best suited the Terrier in me. What I have landed on has more the consistency of a pillow, if you can imagine that.

As I awaken from this deepest of sleeps, up trots a very handsome member of my own species.

"Well, hello there, old chap! Welcome to paradise!"

"Thank you. The name is Duffy, but friends call me Duff."

"Pleased to meet you Duff. I'm Rex."

"Nice to meet you, Rex. I know this may seem like a silly question, and pardon the vernacular, but where in the ..."

EPI-DOGUE
LETTER FROM HOME
(HEAVEN)

The day started off like every other one. Sleep late. Out for a little jog to get the heart pumping. Stand up to a nice big bowl of chow and then find that perfect spot under the big oak tree for a morning nap. Rex had joined me, the two of us lying flat out, the morning sun adding a natural luster to our already shiny coats.

Just about the time that I had found the ideal position certain to bring on that nap, I felt a nudge on my pink belly. It was Ralph the post dog making his daily rounds. To this point in my time up here I had yet to receive any mail, so it startled me a bit when I looked up to see Ralph standing there with a letter personally addressed to me. Eager to find out who could possibly be writing me, I quickly put the envelope between my two paws, tore it open with my incisors, and began reading:

Dear Duff:

   Most parents consider it a miracle when they are present to witness the birth of their children. We may not have been there to witness your birth but we always considered it one of the happiest days of our lives when we brought you home from the shelter. Well, today brought us a second miracle when we saw Duffy: The Tale of a Terrier *on the shelf in our local bookstore. We may never know how it got on that shelf, but that really doesn't matter. What matters is that we now have your complete story to add to the memories we have stored up since the day you left us.*

   Sure, some of the things we remember best are those physical traits that gave you such a handsome appearance:

- *The black and tan head with the stitching on the nose.*

- *The white body sprinkled with black freckles.*

- *The pink belly on the underside.*

- *The ears standing at perfect attention.*

   But other memories are of a different sort:

- *Opening the door from the garage that very first time and you no longer there to greet us.*

- *Months later putting on a pair of pants and finding little strands of bristly white hair.*

- *Seeing the crate tucked away in the basement, the crate that was your home whether you were at home or on the road with us.*

- *Or looking out the window to your doghouse, that wonderful piece of craftsmanship that you found fascinating to visit but not as a substitute for spending your evenings inside with us.*

In the end that is what we are all left with, isn't it? Memories of our times together. Those memories can never be replaced, but we can plant the seeds for new ones. Daisy arrived in our lives a few months after you departed. Just like you, she came to us from a shelter. And just like you, she came with her name. Duffy and Daisy. Begin with a D and end with a Y. But just like what's between the D and the Y, everything else about the two of you is different. You were the rough-and-tumble guy, she the gentle lady. You were always the hard-charging Terrier in the tightly wound suit of white, the ears standing straight up. Daisy is a red-headed Hound with ears that flop. No, Daisy will never replace you, but she can bring that same light to our lives that you did for all those years. And for that we will be forever grateful.

So thanks, Duff, for the memories and for filling in all the missing pieces in your tale. We only wish you could come down for a book-signing, but we realize all miracles have their limits. Our

pictures of you may eventually fade in the light of day, but our memories of you never will.
Love,
Mom and Dad

When I finished reading, I went to swallow but felt a lump in my throat the size of a pig's foot. Rex, sensing that I probably wanted to be alone with my thoughts, quietly trotted down the road. As I folded the letter from home, I looked off to the endless horizon and just knew that, somewhere out there, my folks were thinking of me. But being a dog, I had nowhere on me to tuck my letter from home. So I just tucked it in with all of my other memories and called out to my buddy.

"Hey, Rex. Wait up. I think I've finished my tale."

THE END
(OF THE TALE)

AFTER-DOGUE

They say that time heals. As I write this, it has been exactly five years since Duff left us to join his soon-to-be agent Rex up there. Much like today, it was a cold and blustery winter day when the vet called to say that he was gone.

My wife and I take an exercise class at the local Y. The building happens to share a driveway with the vet's office where Duff spent his last night. This may sound like the lamest excuse in the book for not exercising but, for the longest time after we lost Duff, I had difficulty pulling into the parking lot at the Y. Instinctively, my eyes were always drawn to the window of the vet's office.

I still glance over when we pull into the Y, but at least my eyes no longer fill with tears. I don't know the psychological explanation for the dry eyes, but I suspect it is one of those things that makes us human.

DUFFY

We grieve and then we move on, our memories intact.

You may be wondering how much of Duff's "tale" is true. First and foremost, the part about his tail is anatomically accurate. It was nothing more than a stub. We did adopt him from the local shelter where he had been given his name and where he was in fact Pet of the Week. And it seemed only fitting that the second dog we adopted also came to us with her name, a name that, like Duffy, started with a D and ended with a Y, but with an "ais" in the middle.

We never knew what brought Duff to the shelter. You will have to take his word for it that it involved a farmer with a pitchfork. He literally bounced off the walls when we first went to the shelter to check him out, eager as he was to find a new home.

Yes, Duff did his part to curb the overpopulation problem, passing into neuterhood soon after we adopted him. And unlike some humans who have been known to stretch the truth on their resumes, he did graduate twice from obedience school. Okay, so maybe it was a bit overzealous on his part to refer to his second certificate as an MBA.

Duff watched a lot of years of the Westminster with us. Whether he really dreamed about representing the mixed breeds for Best in Show, I have no idea. You would have to ask him about that.

AFTER-DOGUE

We made a number of moves during Duff's life-time. He grew up a Midwestern dog, already a senior citizen when we moved out West. He did come face to face with a coyote and her pups. He tells the truth when he describes the elk herd out our front window. And I suppose it was fitting that we moved back to the Midwest a few months before he died. His ashes now sit on a shelf in our living room.

And yes, our town really does have a balloon festival. In February. I recall going to watch the launch that weekend after we lost Duff. Our hearts weren't really into it, but we figured it would do us good to get out of the house, away from all the memories. That morning was so cold that the balloons were grounded. It didn't matter. When I looked up to the ice blue sky I could see the lively Bull Terrier up there, gradually floating away from Earth in his very own balloon.

Oh, one more thing. Duff did stay in some fine hotels over his lifetime. And he never smoked, at least not around us. Who knows what he and Rex are doing up there?

—Duff's Dad

ACKNOWLEDGEMENTS

Any dog worth his salt will tell you how dependent he is on humans for his most basic needs: food, shelter, love, affection, rawhides, and chew toys. Throw in the fact that I was a shelter dog and you begin to realize how many people I have to thank.

All animals who have spent time on the inside looking out owe a debt of gratitude to those who helped them find a forever home. So, I start with the good folks at Anderson Animal Shelter in South Elgin, Illinois. They put a roof over my head and most importantly gave me hope that someone out there might be willing to take a chance on Yours Truly. I will always be indebted to my primary care physician, Dr. Roger Mahr, DVM, for all he did to help me live to the ripe old age of fourteen.

How does anyone—human or canine—find the words to thank all those who help him publish his life's story posthumously? I need to start with my biographer, my adopted dad. I had barely reached my heavenly home before he realized how important

it was to get my story out. Along the way, he bene-
fitted from the helpful suggestions of his instructors
and fellow students in various workshops, including
those at the Iowa Summer Writing Festival in Iowa
City and the Loft Literary Center in Minneapolis.

Thanks also to the Phipps Center for the Arts in
Hudson, Wisconsin. The support and encouragement from John Potter, Executive Director, and the
staff at the Phipps were instrumental in bringing my
story to completion. Thanks to Beaver's Pond Press
for seeing the potential in a talking dog story. Marly
Cornell, herself a true friend to the animals, did a
masterful job in editing the manuscript, as did Greg
Holcomb in capturing my very essence in the illustrations. Jay Monroe's design for the book perfectly
complements my story.

Dad may have been the one to put pen to paper,
but he and I both know my story would have never
been told without his wife, my mom. She is the one
who convinced him to go take a look at a lively Bull
Terrier mix in need of a home. She is the one who
put food on the floor for me all those years and saw
to it that I lived a happy and healthy life. And it was
her continual reminders of what determination and
perseverance can do that led to my tale being told.
Thanks, Mom, for your everlasting love.